Not So Fast, Boys . . .

Longarm stared at the captain, his face rigid as granite.

The captain sighed in defeat, shrugging slightly. He glanced over his left shoulder at the men behind him. "All right, fellas. You heard the man. Let her—"

He clipped off the sentence as he jerked his head back toward Longarm, snaking his right hand across his waist for the Colt Army holstered in the cross-draw position on his left hip. At the same time, the other two men suddenly released Arlis, and she hit the floor with a scream just as the captain's Colt came up in a blur of cunning, practiced, quick-draw motion.

He was quick. But he wasn't quick enough to beat a man who already had his own gun drawn and cocked.

Longarm triggered his .44 twice, the explosions making the entire room jump and causing the barman to drop quickly down behind the rough-hewn bar. The captain screamed, stretching his scarred upper lip back from teeth that shone white in the shadows as he stumbled straight toward the stairs.

The other men, now unencumbered by Arlis's flailing flesh, ripped hands toward the hoglegs on their hips. Neither got a gun even half out of its sheath before the lawman's .44 exploded two more times, sending the soldier dancing back toward the stairs and the civilian spinning and flying over a table near the newel post.

TABOR EVANS

LONGARM

AND THE
CROSS FIRE GIRL

JOVE BOOKS, NEW YORK

THE BERKLEY PUBLISHING GROUP
Published by the Penguin Group
Penguin Group (USA) Inc.
375 Hudson Street, New York, New York 10014, USA
Penguin Group (Canada), 90 Eglinton Avenue East, Suite 700, Toronto, Ontario M4P 2Y3, Canada
(a division of Pearson Penguin Canada Inc.)
Penguin Books Ltd., 80 Strand, London WC2R 0RL, England
Penguin Group Ireland, 25 St. Stephen's Green, Dublin 2, Ireland (a division of Penguin Books Ltd.)
Penguin Group (Australia), 250 Camberwell Road, Camberwell, Victoria 3124, Australia
(a division of Pearson Australia Group Pty. Ltd.)
Penguin Books India Pvt. Ltd., 11 Community Centre, Panchsheel Park, New Delhi—110 017, India
Penguin Group (NZ), 67 Apollo Drive, Rosedale, North Shore 0632, New Zealand
(a division of Pearson New Zealand Ltd.)
Penguin Books (South Africa) (Pty.) Ltd., 24 Sturdee Avenue, Rosebank, Johannesburg 2196,
South Africa

Penguin Books Ltd., Registered Offices: 80 Strand, London WC2R 0RL, England

This is a work of fiction. Names, characters, places, and incidents either are the product of the author's imagination or are used fictitiously, and any resemblance to actual persons, living or dead, business establishments, events, or locales is entirely coincidental.

LONGARM AND THE CROSS FIRE GIRL

A Jove Book / published by arrangement with the author

PRINTING HISTORY
Jove edition / June 2011

Copyright © 2011 by Penguin Group (USA) Inc.
Cover illustration by Milo Sinovcic.

ISBN: 978-0-515-14953-1

JOVE®
Jove Books are published by The Berkley Publishing Group,
a division of Penguin Group (USA) Inc.,
375 Hudson Street, New York, New York 10014.
JOVE® is a registered trademark of Penguin Group (USA) Inc.
The "J" design is a trademark of Penguin Group (USA) Inc.

PRINTED IN THE UNITED STATES OF AMERICA

10 9 8 7 6 5 4 3 2 1

Chapter 1

Deputy U.S. Marshal Custis P. Long, known far and wide to friend and foe as Longarm, saw no reason to ever wake up alone. Since each of us was headed for the longest, loneliest sleep of all, there was just no point in enduring a lonesome night or cold, lonely morning on this side of the sod.

Now as he rolled over to find the tight, round rump white as Christmas morning curving against him, he was pleased to see that he'd accomplished his goal once again. The ass moved ever so slightly as the girl breathed, curled on her side beneath the single flannel sheet and two blankets provided by the Burlington Northern rail line to outfit their Pullman cars. *Clickety-clack* went the wheels over the tracks, causing the exquisite rump to nudge Longarm's slumbering dong, which nestled like a fat, brown, pink-headed rodent with its head just barely nudging the girl's crack and the half-moon curve of her love nest.

Cynthia Larimer must have felt the nudge against her

mound, because she gave a dreamy little groan that was just audible above the clatter of the iron wheels. Groggy from his own several hours of shut-eye but feeling instantly aroused by the silky mound tickling the end of his prick, Longarm brushed the girl's long, black hair up above her head and pressed his mouth capped by an untrimmed longhorn mustache against her creamy-smooth neck. At the same time, he slid his left hand up her delectable thigh, dropped it down between her legs, and tucked a finger up against her snatch.

He pushed its tip through the petal-like folds, and worked it around a little.

Cynthia Larimer, the favorite niece of Denver's founding father, General William Larimer, Jr., groaned louder and squirmed, spreading her legs enough that her snatch seemed to suck against the tip of Longarm's finger, inviting it deeper. Longarm obliged the girl. He heard her draw a breath as he buried the finger to its knuckle, then worked it around, feeling the Larimer heiress's fluids oozing against it like warm mud. He kept his lips pressed against her neck, feeling her body temperature rise as he wiggled and waggled his finger, keeping it only knuckle deep to taunt and tease, keep her wanting more.

Cynthia kept her head down, cheek against her pillow, still half-slumbering. She wriggled her ass against him, silently begging him to slide the finger in deeper.

As she did, rubbing against his cock, he felt his own blood warm and begin to engorge his shaft. The impressive organ began to rise like a cannon barrel raised by a winch, bobbing ever so slightly with each beat of the lawman's wicked heart, until it was standing at full mast, the large, purple mushroom head wedged taut between the two pale lobes of the moneyed Miss Cynthia's regal buttocks.

He pulled his finger out.

She groaned like a child who'd had her toy taken away.

Longarm stuck his finger back in, and she groaned in a much higher pitch as the warm honey cache of her snatch sucked at him and oozed so hotly it almost burned his finger. She lifted her head, and in the pearl dawn light pushing through the window beside them, he saw her cobalt-blue eyes regard him through slitted lids. Her wide red lips spread a lusty grin.

"Stop teasing me, you cad," she purred. "Do the proper thing, now, and fuck me."

"Might be getting close to the station."

She'd met him in Las Vegas, New Mexico, after his most recent assignment hunting owlhoots in Texas, and they'd hopped the train together for Denver, where Longarm's boss no doubt waited with another assignment and Cynthia's moneyed Larimer bunch likely waited with a spring dinner and dance in her honor.

"So?"

"Don't wanna get caught with our pants down, Miss Larimer. I'm your 'friend,' remember, and you're the rich girl I escort to the opera from time to time, to keep you out of harm's way amongst your adoring plebeian hordes."

"I'm your little fuck monkey, Custis, and if you don't fuck your little monkey right now and forget about dear Uncle George and Aunt May finding us stuck together here like a couple of dogs, I'm going to scream at the tops of my lungs, and the porters will have quite a story to tell the *Rocky Mountain News*!"

Longarm pulled his finger out and, nibbling her ear-lobe, reached down for his iron-hard staff and slid the unwieldy head between her warm butt cheeks.

"No screaming, monkey."

"Can't promise," she sighed, sucking air through her teeth and grinding her forehead into her pillow.

He found her hungry snatch, the wet lips parted and waiting, and thrust his hips forward. It was Longarm's turn to groan when he felt the silky fur of Cynthia's love nest slide up along the sides of his shaft as the engorged head slid up inside her, farther and farther . . .

Deeper . . . deeper. . . .

Cynthia lifted her chin and opened her mouth.

She squeezed her eyes closed, and a pained expression etched itself on her beautiful china doll face before the lips spread again, wider this time, showing her perfect, porcelain white teeth. Her pink tongue pushed against the front teeth as she stifled a scream that might have brought the porters at a dead run. She reached behind her with one arm and dug her fingers into Longarm's hip as he bottomed out inside her and pressed his nose against the side of her head, sniffing deep of the girl's ripe-cherry fragrance, just the thought of which gave him a raging hard-on when the girl herself was half a world away.

He pulled out of her and slid back in.

Cynthia tossed her head like a mare in season as he continued the maneuver, using the rocking and slight pitching of the train to his best advantage, giving them both a thrill ride that was made ever more thrilling by the vibration of the rail seams up through the bed and into their loins.

When he'd fucked her for five minutes, and she was

chewing her pillowcase to keep from making a racket and ruining her family's reputation, they were nearly falling off the cot. So he wrapped his arm around her flat, soft belly and drew her back toward him, against the car's outside wall and back down over the head of his cock.

The pillowcase slipped out of Cynthia's mouth, and her "Oh, Jesus Fucking Christ!" rose above the hum and clatter of the Pullman, so that as Longarm continued fucking the girl, really thrusting now and battering her backside with his hips, he clamped his own hand across her mouth. He felt her sharp little teeth, wet lips, and hot breath against his palm, and this aroused him further, so that he slipped over into that netherworld of penultimate carnal bliss.

He squeezed his eyes closed, kneaded her breasts with his hands, curled his toes, and gritted his teeth.

A full two agonizing minutes later—two minutes that would have killed a man even slightly less fit than Longarm—and knowing that Cynthia was at the apex of her own fiery rise, he released a jet of super-pressurized jism deep into the girl's expanding and contracting bowels.

Cynthia screamed into his palm. The scream lasted nearly a minute. When it died, she went to whimpering and licking his hand like a puppy.

His spasms as well as hers diminished to the easy jostling one might encounter on a slow ride in a simple farm wagon, and Longarm lay back against the bed. Hands clamped over the girl's two firm breasts, he drew her taut against him. Her jutting nipples pricked his palms like acorns. He nuzzled her neck, licked her jaw.

Cynthia groaned and reached up to place a hand on his unshaven cheek. "Custis, you bastard, no man knows how to bring a woman off quite like you."

Longarm chuckled immodestly. "No need for such farm talk, Miss Larimer."

"I can only use such talk with you." She snaked a hand down and caressed his ball sack with her fingertips. "Do you think we can do it again real soon?"

Longarm chuckled again. He was about to reply that he'd haul the sex-crazed debutante's ashes anytime she liked, but then he closed his mouth and lifted his head from her neck, eyes narrowing curiously. In the tumult of the last several minutes, he hadn't noticed the train slowing. But now he could feel the jerks as the brakemen applied the brakes to all the cars, and the long, shrill whistle rose like a goddess's love scream.

With an expression of disbelief, he lifted his head farther and drew the shade up from the dusty, soot-streaked window. He'd recognize those corrals and stock-loading chutes lining the tracks anywhere—an entire maze of them, some empty, some filled with milling cattle and several mustached, quirley-smoking cowboys regarding the train in their grim, dull-eyed fashion.

The Burlington flier was pulling into Denver's Union Station.

"Oh, shit."

"What is it?" Cynthia groaned, wriggling her incredible ass against his balls.

"We're in Denver."

"So we're in Denver," the girl said, her voice thickening as though she were about fall into an exhausted slumber. "That's where we've been heading, my dear

Custis. Now, if I can pull myself together and walk like a lady after that pummeling you just gave me, we'll just head on over to the Larimer Hotel and get down to the same kind of business—"

She broke off abruptly and lifted her head. "Oh, god, Uncle George and Aunt May said they were going to meet my train!"

"Our train, you mean," Longarm said darkly.

Just as he turned his head to peer up the tracks toward the locomotive that was filling the skies with black smoke and glowing cinders, among the milling throngs upon the cobblestone platform of the forever-bustling Union Station, he saw, as though his dread-filled mind had conjured them of its own accord, the general and Mrs. Larimer looking old and gray but somehow still dashing and exclusive in their tailored duds, the general smoking a cigar the size of a dynamite stick, Aunt May holding a silk parasol.

Cynthia craned her neck to give him a dire look.

"Any chance they might be expectin' to see us together?" he asked.

"I could come up with a lie as to how we found ourselves on the same train *unexpectedly*," Cynthia whispered as the train jerked and ground to a final halt. She swallowed and smiled wanly. "But I don't know how we could explain being found together in my sleeping compartment."

"I reckon we'd best not let 'em find us here, then," Longarm said, scrambling over the still-lounging Larimer debutante and climbing down off the bed.

He began gathering his clothes, which he and Cynthia had strewn about the tiny compartment with her

own, after supping together last night in the dining car
and snuggling for a time in the observation car, watching
the stars and steeling little, proscribed feels when no
porters or ticket agents were around. When they'd worked
themselves into a lustful frenzy, they'd hurried here to
undress each other and do dirty things into the wee hours
of the morning.

The car rocked and swayed as the other passengers
detrained. Cynthia peeked out the window, keeping her
head low and turning sharply to look up toward the
locomotive. She gasped.

"Oh, god, Custis—Uncle George isn't on the platform. Just Aunt May!"

"Maybe he went for a hot dog," Longarm dryly muttered as he stumbled around, pulling on his long handles
with one hand while reaching under the bed for his
tobacco-tweed trousers with the other.

"He's come looking for me!"

"You best get dressed, maybe."

Longarm paused to admire the vision of the naked
girl sitting up in the middle of the small folding bed—
rich black hair in a tumbling mess upon her shoulders,
framing her perfect, white, pear-shaped breasts, which
were still slightly chafed from Longarm's brushy mustache. "Unless you think we can hide in here and go on
up to Cheyenne. Might kill each other before we could
turn around and come back, but, girl, I can't think of a
better way to go!"

"Oh, Custis!"

Longarm sat down on the bed to finish pulling on his
long handles. "Well, get dressed, girl! Break a leg! Sooner
we can head on out there, separate, the sooner we can

forestall your aunt and uncle finding out we've been doing more than just tramping around Denver enjoying the theater and them consarned symphonies of yours."

Cynthia shot him an indignant look. "*'Consarned'?*"

Then, the direness of the situation slamming her like a sledge, she bolted forward as though shot from a cannon, and scrambled off the bed. Stumbling around each other like drunken dancers at a remote cavalry camp on New Year's Eve, they gathered their clothes and dressed. Outside the sleeping compartment door, there was a sickening lack of sound. The other train passengers had likely all left the car by now, which would make it much easier for General Larimer to find the Pullman compartment containing his lovely niece . . . and her unsanctioned lover.

Longarm was in his shirt and trousers and reaching for his cartridge belt and double-action Colt Frontier .44 when voices sounded outside the compartment. Men's voices. He recognized the voice of the porter, Malcolm Murray, and the deep, rumbling baritone of the General himself. The voices grew louder as the men approached Cynthia's compartment.

A stone dropped in Longarm's belly. Cynthia froze as she sat on the bed, trying to cover her wonderful breasts with a lacy, red and pink corset.

A knock on the door. The General cleared his throat. "Oh, Cynthia? Cynthia, dear, it's Uncle George . . . !"

Cynthia looked at Longarm. It was the look of one condemned prisoner turning to the another as they stood upon a gallows with hangman's knots being tightened behind their necks.

Chapter 2

Knock-knock-knock.

"Cynthia, dear! Oh, Cynthia! The young porter here says this is your compartment. Are you awake?"

Cynthia was still staring at Longarm as though await- ing a trapdoor beneath her feet to open. Longarm, who'd been at war with bad guys of every stripe and even a few angry bears and bobcats, wanted no trouble with Den- ver's founding father. The federal lawman, while occa- sionally fed up with his oft-hectic job that gave him little time for play, was far from ready to start mucking out livery stalls for a living. And that's what he'd likely be doing if Cynthia's uncle got wind of the fact that his fa- vorite niece was being boned regularly by a forty-a-month wage-earning government badge-toter.

It was of course no secret that all the Larimers were expecting Cynthia to marry—whenever the precocious, young, artsy, globe-trotting debutante finally decided to settle down—someone perched on the same rung of the socioeconomic ladder as she was. One or two rungs higher, all the better!

But a good ten or fifteen rungs lower was not only out of the question, it would likely get the poor fella shot with one of Uncle George's foreign-built bird guns.

Holding his breath as well as a sock in one hand, his dangling cartridge belt in the other, Longarm frowned at the tongue-tied Cynthia and canted his head impatiently at the door. Cynthia cleared her throat, a flush rising high in her regal, tapering cheeks, to which curls of her black hair clung.

"Uh . . . um . . . good morning, Uncle George. I . . . I was just waking up. So sorry. I'll be out in a minute."

"Good heavens, dear—you gave me a start," the general said with disapproval. "I was about to have the young porter here kick your door down!"

"Oh, no—don't do that, Uncle," Cynthia said, trying to pitch her voice with humor but coming off only clumsy and nervous as she cut her desperate eyes between Longarm and the thin width of door that separated her and the half-dressed lawdog from the hell on the other side. "Go on back out to the platform, please. It'll take me a minute to gather my things."

"Open the door, dear, and I'll have the porter help you."

Cynthia jerked a palm-out hand at the door. "Oh, no! That's all right. I'm not even dressed yet. I'll be out soon, Uncle George. And then I'll summon the porter for help."

"Nonsense," said Uncle George. "He and I will wait for you right here. No more dallying, now, Cynthia. Aunt May is waiting just outside the car. We have a table reserved at the Larimer Hotel. Want to take you to lunch, you see . . ."

"Of course, of course," Cynthia said to the door, bending forward a little and wringing her hands together as though praying her uncle couldn't see through the slender width of wood that separated him from her and her lover. "Thank you, Uncle George. I'll be out in just a few minutes!"

She glanced at Longarm, her eyes wide with trepidation but also sparkling slightly with the thrill of their having once more been nearly caught in the act of their proscribed frolic. Longarm chuckled dryly under his breath as he continued to dress, cat-footed and quiet. The girl was a daredevil, he'd give her that. But then, he'd known that all along. Hadn't she given him a blow-job beneath the general's very own desk in Larimer Hall during a Christmas ball two years ago? . . . While the general and Longarm's boss, Chief Marshal Billy Vail, had conversed with Longarm—who'd been sitting in the general's chair with his fly open and his enormous boner jutting up into Cynthia's sweet, sucking mouth—from only a few feet away?!

Longarm chuckled again as he grabbed his black frock coat off a chair back and shrugged into it. He slipped his string tie around his neck and then paused to watch Cynthia pull her stockings up her long, slender, porcelain-pale legs. She still hadn't tied her corset, and her firm, pale breasts were jostling to and fro as though trying to entice the lawman into giving her another good pummeling even as Denver's founding father waited for her just outside the door . . .

Cynthia, her cheeks pink with excitement, gave him a

sparkling grin and a sidelong smile, reading his mind.
Christ, even in such a prickly situation as this, the blue-
eyed, stygian-haired succubus could still give him a hard-
on. She knew it, too, because after she'd pulled her green
velvet cape around her shoulders and stuffed her little
straw hat into her canvas accordion grip, letting her hur-
riedly brushed hair hang freely to her shoulders, she
turned to him, let her fingers flutter devilishly against his
crotch, and pressed her ripe mouth against his once more,
nibbling his lower lip.

"Soon, Custis?" she purred.

"If I haven't died from heatstroke," he grunted as his
loins surged hotly, tingling, under the black magic of her
lingering hand on his tightening crotch. "I'll look you
up, Miss Larimer."

"Perhaps dinner at Larimer Hall? I'll finagle you an
invite, and we can do dirty things in Uncle George's
office-library again."

She snickered. Longarm glowered, but she didn't
wait for his response. She nibbled his lip once more,
gave him that glittering, sidelong grin, then opened the
door a crack to poke her head out into the car. "Uncle
George!" she squealed.

She hurried out and shut the door behind her, and
then Longarm waited, feeling his crotch loosen gradually, his heart cease throbbing, while she and Uncle George
greeted each other exuberantly, their voices drifting off
to murmurs that soon were absorbed by the general din
of the station platform.

Longarm chuckled, relieved, and dug into the pocket
of his hickory shirt for one of the three-for-a-nickel che-

roots he bought in handfuls whenever he was in Denver, keeping a good four or five close to hand at all times. He dug a Lucifer out of his pants, scratched it to life on his thumbnail, and, chuckling once more and shaking his head at the closeness of his most recent call with General Larimer, touched fire to cigar.

Puffing smoke, he blew out the match, flipped it away, then dropped to his knees to dig his McClellan saddle, saddlebags, and prized Winchester '73 rifle out from beneath the low-slung folding bed. When he'd retrieved all the gear, he left-shouldered the saddlebags and saddle and right-shouldered the rifle, keeping the long gun in his dominant hand out of long habit of potential need, as he fumbled open the sleeping compartment door and stepped out into the aisle between other such compartments, all of which smelled musty with the pent-up human smells of sweat, leather, and wool, as well as the stench of the animals—chickens, waterfowl, and dogs, mostly—that some folks traveled with.

He was glad for the cigar.

Looking along the aisle, toward the front of the car, he saw no sign of either Cynthia or her uncle, but, wanting to make sure he saw neither again until he was good and ready, he started along the aisle toward the car's rear, puffing the stogie and enjoying the sweet memories of his and Cynthia's tryst. It had been a short-lived run, but then most of theirs were, and it was not the time spent together, he reminded himself, but the quality of that time.

And last night on the train making its way up along the side of the star-mantled Sangre de Cristo, with a balmy breeze smelling of sage and spring wildflowers whispering through the windows, was right up there with their best time of all.

Longarm went out into the sleeping car's vestibule. Clamping the cigar in his teeth and balancing the cavalry kak and saddlebags on his left shoulder, he clamped that hand over the brass rail running up the car's three steps, and leaned forward to peer up in the direction in which Cynthia and her aunt and uncle might be. Spying none of the Larimers there in the milling crowd up thataway, Longarm released his hand from the rail and used it to steady his gear, puffing the stogie as he made his way down off the Pullman car and onto the cobbled platform. There were a half dozen men and women dressed for travel shuffling around him, one black porter with a squawky-wheeled luggage cart, and a shaggy-headed little boy in a watch cap hawking the morning edition of the *Rocky Mountain News*.

So he didn't see the short brunette in a gray duster and tan hat clutching a wooden-handled .36 Smith & Wesson, until she stepped out around the luggage cart, raising the little Smithy while cocking it, bunching her red lips, and setting her hazel eyes on fire as she squealed at Longarm, "Die, killer, die!"

The Smithy popped, belching smoke and fire.

Chapter 3

The bullet fired by the man-dressed brunette made a little scritching sound as it sliced across the top of Longarm's shoulder-mounted McClellan.

The second bullet felt like a toothpick poked at the outside edge of his right ear before it barked off a brass rail of the Pullman car behind him, then screeched off God knew where. The girl was trying to cock the little popper once more when Longarm, bolting forward, sliced the smoking Smithy away from his face with his Winchester's barrel. Continuing forward with the force of his own momentum, he plowed right on through the girl, sending her stumbling straight back off her boot heels.

Both he and she continued up and over the porter's luggage cart, knocking over the ten or fifteen trunks and carpetbags and sending the entire stack spilling down around them as they themselves hit the cobbles on the cart's other side.

In the tangle-up, Longarm lost his battle-scarred saddle and saddlebags but managed to hold on to the Winchester as, with his left hand, he grabbed a shoulder of the struggling girl and shoved her back down onto the tobacco-stained platform.

"Let go of me, you bastard!" the girl screamed. "I'll kill you! I'll kill you! You lyin', cheatin', murderin' sonofabitch!" She grunted and groaned as she tried to slither out from under the long, broad drink of water that was Longarm—standing, she couldn't have come up much beyond his brisket—while reaching for the Smithy cooling on the cobbles near a seldom-used crate sandbox receptacle for chaw, cigarette, and cigar butts. "I'll kill you!"

"I don't think so, you little demon!" Longarm's ear burned, and his dander was up. He'd been bushwhacked before, but it always rubbed him the wrong way something fierce, and it didn't matter if it was perpetrated by seasoned, unshaven killers or little killers. He managed to slam her back down hard against the cobbles, straddling her on his knees, and pinned her right arm down with the butt of his Winchester, her left arm down with his own right.

"I don't, either, Longarm," said a boy's voice, and Longarm glanced to his right to see the little newspaper hawker holding up the girl's still smoking Smithy in his dirty little hand and grinning like the cat that ate the canary. "I got her gun, and she won't it get back from me, nohow!"

"Obliged, Teddy," Longarm growled, scowling down at the girl still struggling beneath him. "Hold on to it for me, will you?"

"You got it, Longarm! You gonna fill her full o' hot

lead? She done tried to drill ya, after all. I seen the whole thing!" The boy was flushed with eager cheer.

"Give it here, you dirty little urchin!" the girl barked at Teddy. "I'm going to kill your friend Longarm here, send him off to Jesus with a bullet through each eye and another through his black heart!"

The girl's ferocity was so off-putting that Longarm felt his own rage at the nearly successful drygulching sputter and pop like water on a hot stove lid. "Good lord, girl," he said, frown lines slicing across his forehead and slitting his brown eyes. "Why in the hell are you so damn determined to blow my lamp?"

She quit struggling to glare up at him with her hazel eyes that would have been right pretty on any other pretty girl who hadn't nearly drilled a third eye through his head. "Because you killed my father, you bastard. Maybe not yourself, no! But you as good as killed him. Got him hung in front of the whole cowardly town of Wagon Mound!" Tears varnished the girl's eyes, and her smooth, lightly tanned cheeks mottled red-and-white as unbridled grief tainted her rage. "And you told him you'd make sure that never happened!"

Longarm's scowl cut deeper, and dread pitched his voice. "What's your name?"

The girl choked back a sob, trying hard to keep looking tough. "Arlis Pine."

A stone dropped in Longarm's belly. He opened his mouth to speak once more but held back when clacking footsteps rose above the hum of the station crowd gathered in a semicircle around Longarm, Arlis Pine, and the scattered luggage. No one looked more incredulous than the black porter, who'd been pushing the luggage cart and who, like the newsboy, had seen the entire bush-whacking and was likely judging his own distance from one of those two ricochets.

A voice attached itself to the clacking footsteps, and a blue-uniformed policeman broke through the crowd, red-faced between shaggy cinnamon muttonchops. "What the hell's goin'. . . ?" Police Sergeant Hannibal Kennedy stopped before Longarm and Miss Pine, holding a police-model Colt .44 in his ham-sized, freckled right fist. "Custis?"

He stared down, as incredulous as the newsboy, the porter, and the rest of the crowd. Sergeant Kennedy slid his puzzled, watery blue eyes—he'd likely been having a beer in the Black Cat Saloon across Wyandot Street from the big sandstone station when he'd heard the shots—between the girl and the big man pinning her down.

Longarm removed his rifle stock from the girl's arm, and she gave a little yowl at the suddenly released pressure and yanked her other hand free to grab the arm and rub it. "It's all right, Hannibal," Longarm said, still scrutinizing the girl but ready to grab her if she went for another weapon. "Just a little misunderstanding, I think."

"No misunderstandin', mister," the girl said, shaking her head slowly. Her voice was softer now but just as taut, determined, and teeming with acrimony. She knew she'd lost the battle, but the war was still up for grabs. Bitterly, eyes nearly crossed with barely bridled rage, she continued: "I understood real good and sound that you left my pa alone up there in Wagon Mound, right where Del Sager and that gun-heavy bunch of polecats he rides with could find him . . . and hang him from the same tree Sager himself should have been hanged from only last year. Only, you an' the judge said no, you couldn't hang him because you didn't have enough evidence to prove he was guilty. Better send him to jail. Ha!"

The girl's caustic laugh was loud as a shot from her little Smithy. "Well, that jail didn't hold him, just like Sager said it wouldn't. And he came back to Wagon Mound and he killed my pa just like he promised he would."

"Ah, Christ." Longarm ran a forearm across his brow as he felt another cold stone drop in his belly. "Your pa's Alvin Pine, isn't he?"

The girl said, "At least Sager kept his word. Better'n you done, you mangy cayuse of a no-good lawdog. You promised you'd make sure my pa was kept safe from Sager's bunch and from Sager himself, once Sager got out of prison. Well, here you are in Denver all duded up in your black frock coat and your tweed trousers, smoking a cheap cigar and tippin' your hat to the ladies."

She sucked a sharp, soggy breath, then half-screamed and half-cried, "While my pa's done turnin' to dirt in his pine-board coffin!"

Her head sagged back against the cobbles as she gave in to a long fit of bawling, covering her eyes with her arm. Her shoulders quivered, flat belly sucking in and out behind her wool plaid shirt. Longarm rose slowly from the girl, feeling wretched. She was right. He had told the town marshal of Wagon Mound, Wyoming Territory, that he'd make sure no harm came to him when Del Sager got free. But he sure as hell had never expected Sager to get free so quickly.

A prison break, eh? Had to be.

With a ragged sigh, feeling more stunned than anything else by all that had just happened and what he'd learned, Longarm plucked the .36 Smith & Wesson out of the newsboy's grubby, ink-stained hands. He flipped the kid a quarter but felt no lightening of spirits from the glow the coin put in the working lad's young eyes.

"Want me to take her in, Custis?" Kennedy asked as part of the crowd dispersed, heading off toward waiting trains, while others remained, frowning and conversing among themselves, regarding the crying girl lying on the cobbles with the voyeuristic curiosity of Peeping Toms.

Longarm shook his head. "Let's let this one go, eh, Han?"

Kennedy nodded, chewing his lip and holstering his six-shooter. "I reckon we can at that. She looks plum miserable." The policeman gave Longarm a sidelong glance. "She did try to clean your clock, though, you know? And might've hit a bystander with a ricochet."

"Let's let it go, Han. Can you do that?"

"I reckon I couldn't hear the shots. Lots of coal wagons thundering down Wyandot Street this time of the morning, don't you know?" Kennedy gave a feeble smile. The egg he'd had with a schooner of beer was fringing his mustache. "And I'd hate to lock one up as young and pretty as that one there. They don't stay young and pretty for long in the city lockup, you know."

"Obliged to you, Han."

Longarm stuffed the Smithy behind his cartridge belt, and went over to the girl, while Kennedy hazed the crowd away from her and the spilled luggage. The porter had begun picking up some of the luggage with the air of a man toying too close to a rattlesnake hole, casting the girl quick, skeptical glances.

Squatting, Longarm hooked his arms beneath Arlis Pine's and hauled her to her feet. She was still sobbing, and she tried to resist Longarm's help, but he'd hauled her up too fast. She looked a little shocked to find herself standing, and glanced around quickly to get her bearings, then turned her eyes, like two balls of molten sulfur, on the lawman once more. She opened her mouth to speak, then clamped her jaws shut once more. Casting him one more dark glare through slitted eyes, she bent down to scoop her hat off the cobbles.

Longarm hooked his thumbs behind his cartridge belt and rocked back on the low heels of his mule-eared cavalry boots. "Were you gonna hop one of these cars after you'd given me a window I hadn't ordered?"

"No!"

"What were you gonna do, then?"

"I hadn't gotten that far," she said and pouted.

Longarm turned to the newsboy, who'd begun hawking papers once again, walking slowly up and down the cobbles. "Teddy, can you spare a few more minutes? There'll be another quarter in it for you."

"Sure!" The boy grinned.

"Stow my gear in a locker here, will you? Give the key to Ned Castle. He's the supervising ticket agent. I'll retrieve it from him."

"You got it, Longarm."

The lawman tossed another coin to the boy, who snapped it expertly out of the air. The boy scrutinized the silver button and polished it on a leg of his patched knickers before reaching down for the lawman's Winchester where it had piled up beside an iron-banded steamer trunk.

Longarm grabbed the girl's arm and began leading her away from the train. He hoped Cynthia and her moneyed aunt and uncle were far from Union Station as he entered the cool, airy, high-ceilinged building that always smelled like sweat and, inexplicably, licorice. He didn't want to have to deal with them now on the heels of this. Arlis Pine tried to pull away from him, but he kept his left hand clamped on her slender arm, squeezing harder the more she fought him, till she gave a little yowl and held his stride, sort of skip-hopping to keep up, her duster flapping out behind her.

"Where you taking me, damn you?"

"To see my boss. Really don't know what else to do with you. If I let you go, you're liable to try to clean my clock again before I can run down Del Sager and the rest of your father's killers."

"It's a little late for that, mister. The killing was three weeks ago, and the Sager gang is long gone. I tracked 'em—I was the only one with balls enough around Wagon Mound to try it—but they kept to the rockiest ground they could find. The bastards are good, I'll give them that. Didn't find one warm horse apple."

Longarm stopped outside the front of Union Station, and the girl clamped her hat down on her head as the wind plucked at it. "So, like I said, don't bother. You weren't there when my pa needed you, you bastard. It's too late. The Sager bunch is high in the Cheyenne Mountains, screwin' and drinkin' and braggin' around the minin' camps about how they sprung Del from the federal lockup and killed the town marshal who put 'im there!"

Longarm waved to the mustached driver of a parked hansom cab, who was reading one of Teddy's still-damp newspapers. As the man closed his paper and grabbed his reins off the cab's brake handle, Longarm looked down at the pretty, hard, tanned, tear-streaked face of Arlis Pine. "Look, I'm real sorry about your pa. Truly I am. But right now I'd like for you to do one thing for me."

She cocked one booted foot and crossed her arms on her chest. "What's that?"

"Shut up."

Chapter 4

Longarm was surprised that Arlis Pine obeyed his order and kept her mouth shut as the cab sputtered up the gentle rise of Sixteenth Street, the horse's shod hooves clomping hollowly along the cobbles, the cab itself jerking to and fro as the driver made his way around lumber drays and beer wagons parked before warehouses and saloons lining both sides of the narrow street in the thundering heart of Denver.

Twice they stopped for a streetcar with its bell clanging, and then once for a gaggle of ladies dressed to the nines in spring-weight frocks and feathered picture hats—the Denver Opera's board of directors. Cynthia had pointed them out to the rangy lawman once before, on one of the opera nights that he endured for the carnal delights she rewarded him with, not the least of which was once a handjob in the governor's private box, with the governor himself and the first lady sitting in front of

Longarm and Cynthia, who'd been wearing long, white silk gloves.

The opera's board of directors met each Thursday morning at the Larimer Hotel for tea and pound cake and to impress one another with their knowledge of worldly culture, as well to discuss opera funding, Cynthia had pointed out. But mostly to see and be seen, and quite a site they were, Longarm observed absently as the cab hammered past them, dressed as they were in enough ruffled muslin, crinoline, lace, fake flowers, and gawdy ostrich feathers to outfit half the soiled doves in Leadville. Quite a startling contrast to the moody, crestfallen urchin slumped down in the seat beside Longarm—a pretty girl, but dusty and sad and smelling like horse sweat and gunsmoke, and with revenge chewing away at her mind.

Arlis Pine belonged to a world these women had never experienced—the renegade frontier up Wyoming way, especially up around the Pumpkin Buttes and the little town of Lightning Flat, in Crazy Woman County, where life was decidedly more rugged and dangerous than anything these opera ladies had ever, could ever imagine. Up there at the edge of the Belle Fourche badlands, a man's life was worth little more than that of a rattlesnake skin. In fact, Longarm had seen a man shot for such a skin up there once, in a dugout stage relay station—shot for the diamondback skin he'd used for a hatband, and for no other reason than that the burly, drunken buffalo hunter liked the way the decoration looked and wanted to give it to the Indian whore he'd just poked over a rain barrel out back of the place.

This was before Longarm had become a federal badge-toter, of course—just a snip still dazed from his bloody experience in the War Between the States, and too shocked at the killing to have done anything about it but gape and wake up with nightmares over it for several months later. That had been a long time ago, but Longarm had been through that country since several times—the last when he'd sat in on the trial of Del Sager for shooting a circuit judge and then hanging the man and shooting him again, over and over, until he looked like something that buzzards had been feeding on for days.

Now a good man—and there were damn few good men in that Pumpkin Butte country—was dead up there. A good lawman named Alvin Pine. And, if the late Lightning Flat marshal's high-blooded, bereaved daughter had her facts straight, Sager's gang was running wild in the Bear Lodge Mountains, celebrating a good man's demise. And Longarm would have to ride in and pull them out to answer for their crimes.

But what about Longarm's own crime? Now that he'd had time to think over what he'd learned, and Arlis had held her tongue while sitting there stewing in the anticlimax of her fury-driven shooting attempt on a federal lawman, he found himself trying to answer for his own sin—namely, going back on his word to Alvin Pine that he'd make sure Del Sager did not make good on his promise to kill Pine for testifying at Sager's court trial.

The cab pulled up in front of the Federal Building. Longarm got out and reached in for Arlis Pine, who continued to slump in the hide-covered seat, her hat mashed down on a knee, glowering at him now with not so much fury as incredulity. "Where the hell you takin' me?" She looked out the door and appraised the big brick building behind him from beneath brows a shade lighter than her hair. "I was here yesterday, and I didn't like it none. No one here helped me or my pa any better than you did."

"Like I said at the train station, I'm gonna hold on to you till I can figure out what to do with you."

"Oh, don't worry—I promise not to try shootin' you again. I'm a damn good shot with that Smithy. That you're still kickin' must mean the Good Lord or whoever the hell is in charge has got it more in for me than you." She extended a dirty hand. "Can I just please have my pistol back? I'll be on my way. I got chickens to feed back at the ranch."

"What ranch?"

"The Cross Fire Ranch. Me and my pa's little spread outside of Lightning Flat. I got the neighbor woman tendin' my stock, but since Pa's dead now, thanks to you, there's only me to do the work around the place. And the work there in that dry country is considerable."

Another Apache war lance of guilt drilled Longarm through the spleen. Christ, she was alone up there now. Working a ranch alone. She couldn't have been much over sixteen, if that. What would become of such a child?

While she was crusty as a week-old loaf of brown bread, there was a tender innocence about her. That was evident in the crazy fact of her coming here, intending to give Longarm what she believed was his rightful reckoning since she could not hunt down the men who'd actually killed her father in Lightning Flat. He supposed such a plan made sense to her, as it likely would to anyone from that woolly country. Folks up there lived by a different set of rules—the same rules that had governed the entire frontier not all that long ago.

"I'm a fool," Longarm growled. "But not that big a fool. Get out here, or I'll throw the cuffs on you and haul you up to the chief marshal's office like a bag of cracked corn on my shoulder."

The girl protested more, but in the end she must have realized that the federal badge-toter had a good foot in height on her, and a hundred pounds in weight, and that he'd restrained bigger prisoners than she. She crouched out the cab's door and waited impatiently on the curb while Longarm paid the driver.

As the cab rattled away, the federal lawman led the girl up the broad marble steps that now, just after business hours had started, were relatively deserted. A couple of federal prosecuting attorneys had stopped to converse about halfway up the steps while holding leather grips under their arms and smoking dynamite-sized stogies. Both men, whom Longarm knew, nodded at him and gave the curious eye to the pretty but ragged, sullen girl he led along by one elbow.

"My niece," Longarm dryly quipped. "Visiting from back east, don't ya know."

The two men glanced skeptically at each other as Longarm held one of the large, wooden doors open for Miss Pine. A few minutes later, he opened the door on the third floor that announced CHIEF MARSHAL DENVER FIRST DISTRICT in gold-leaf lettering, and hazed the girl into Billy Vail's outer office ahead of him. Just inside, Billy Vail's prissy, bespectacled secretary, Henry, was playing his typing machine with a vengeance, as he usually was, slowing down only slightly as he glanced over his shoulder at Longarm.

"You're early, Marshal Long . . ." Henry let his voice

trail off and lifted his hands from the typing machine's keys as he allowed his gaze from behind the round, thick lenses of his glasses to linger on the girl. "And you brought a . . . uh . . . *guest.*"

"Henry, this is Miss Pine. Miss Pine—"

"We've met," she said in a droll, impatient tone.

"Yes." Henry sniffed and thumbed his glasses up his nose, looking confused in that prissy, haughty way only Henry could look—beleaguered and defensive about things not adding up. "Yesterday . . . Thought you must have gone home, Miss Pine."

Before the girl could answer, Longarm said, "The chief in?"

"Yes, but he wasn't expecting you till this afternoon. Didn't your train just get in?"

"Indeed it did." To the girl, Longarm said, "Have a seat, Miss Pine."

She crossed her arms on her chest. "I'll stand."

"All right." Longarm grabbed his handcuffs off the back of his cartridge belt and quickly, before the girl could make another fuss, closed one cuff around her left wrist and expertly closed the other one around a branch of the hat tree beside her. "There—that oughta hold you."

"Hey—damn you!"

"Deputy Long—what is the meaning of this?" Henry said, astounded by Longarm's poor treatment of the pretty young girl from Lightning Flat.

"Just keep an eye on her." Longarm headed for the frosted glass-paneled door flanking the secretary's desk and on which CHIEF MARSHAL VAIL was stenciled in typically unadorned government script. "If she tries to go anywhere with that hat tree, give a yell."

He left Henry hemming and hawing and the girl stewing, one cuffed hand raised to the hat tree above her shoulder, and knocked twice on Billy Vail's door. He shoved the door open without waiting for an invitation.

Chief Marshal Vail sat behind his large, cluttered desk, looking toward the door through a customary cloud of cheap tobacco smoke. Vail was a pudgy, balding, bespectacled man in his fifties. Round-faced and drawn, his features at once craggy and pale, he was a man you never would have guessed had once been anything more than a pencil-pusher. In fact, he'd been quite the sand-crawed law-bringer in his day. Almost as good as Longarm, though some might have said he'd been even better, in even gnarlier times than these.

Now he just looked tired and fat as he blinked owlishly behind his thick glasses and took another deep puff from the stogie wedged between two plump fingers, saying raspingly while blowing smoke through his nostrils, "Ah, fuck, too early for you, Longarm. I wasn't expecting you till this afternoon."

"Never too early for me, Chief."

"I'm feeling a little dyspeptic."

"Rough night?"

"Wife's sister and brother-in-law came to visit with their four howling brats. Why couldn't you have slept in this morning of all mornings?" Vail frowned, waved at the cigar smoke swirling thickly around his big, round head with its receding, sandy hairline. "Wait a minute— didn't your train just pull in? Figured you'd be hoofing it back to the poor side of Cherry Creek."

"I was almost carried feet first out of the train station and over to a marble slab at the local undertaker's. If it wasn't for Lady Luck smiling down on me this fine Colorado morning, you'd be crying real tears 'bout now."

"I doubt that." Vail stared, incredulous, and sagged back in his chair. His string tie curved down over his potbelly sheathed in a wrinkled white shirt, the sleeves of which were rolled up his fishbelly-white forearms. "What happened?"

"Let's just say the daughter of Alvin Pine came to collect on a bill."

"Arlis Pine? She was just in here yesterday."

"So she said."

"You mean she . . . ?" Billy let his voice trail off, and his brows bent as he figured it out. "You gotta be shittin' me. That little girl tried to snuff your wick down at the train station?"

"Ain't she a caution? Thanks for informing the little assassin when my train was due!"

Vail coughed to cover a dry chuckle. "Well, shit, Custis—I sure never expected that little . . . that little girl . . . to go off half-cocked!" He coughed again.

"Oh, she didn't go off half-cocked. She had that little Smithy at full-cock, and all cylinders showed brass."

"You all right?"

"Like I said, Lady Luck . . . I reckon Alvin Pine didn't fair so good."

"Ah, Christ."

Vail's mood changed drastically. He shuffled through a stack of folders on the left side of his desk, found one, and tossed it onto the side of the desk facing Longarm, who sagged down into the red Morocco leather visitor's chair.

The chief marshal said, "The news about Sager's jailbreak came just after you left for New Mexico on the trail of them army deserters with the stolen Gatling guns. I saw no reason to cut your mission short, because it wasn't but the very next day I got word that Sager had already gathered his gang and ridden back to Wyoming and murdered Alvin Pine."

"Goddamnit all, Billy." Longarm tossed his hat down on the edge of the chief marshal's desk. "You tellin' me that cutthroat gang has got a whole three-week lead on me, and there's been no law on their trail all this time?"

"Hold your water, for chrissakes, Custis. You ain't the only badge-toter in my stable, you know. I sent Burt Frieze up there. Last I heard he was in a little backwater on the Galvin and Anderson spur line, about a week behind Sager."

"Frieze, huh?" Longarm nodded his approval. "Good man. But that don't mean he don't need help. Whatever you got for me, it'll have to wait till I've done seen Sager hung like he shoulda been hanged in the first damned place."

"That's what I got for you. Knew you wouldn't take no for an answer." Vail tapped ashes into an overflowing ashtray. "I hate to see you take it so hard, Custis. This kinda thing happens, you know. Lawmen die every day out here."

"But this lawman I promised to help out if I got word Sager had shook free of his federal bridle. Goddamnit, Billy, I promised the man this wouldn't happen. Alvin Pine was all alone up there, the nearest sheriff pret' near a hundred miles away and a drunkard to boot!"

"You made the promise because you wanted Sager locked up, and that judge from Laramie wouldn't hang his rancid hide because there were no eyewitnesses to his murder of the other judge from Chugwater. Pine had been on the Sager bunch's trail at the time and knew there was no one else who could have done the dirty deed."

Vail loosed another cloud toward the window on his left and fanned the smoke with his hand. "It just goes to reason. You couldn't have predicted the son of a two-peso *puta* would break out of the federal lockup in Julesburg in *one year's time*. No way to foresee such a thing. That's the first break they've had in nine years! Shake it off, now, damnit."

"I can't shake it off. His daughter's in the outer office with Henry, and I got her shackled to your hat tree. And she's one awful pitiful sight—I'll tell you, Billy!"

Vail turned his swivel chair sideways and ran a pudgy hand down his face in frustration. "I know—I met her yesterday." He cast a sidelong look at Longarm. "What're you gonna do with her? Poor, pitiful thing did try to clean your clock, you know, Custis."

"I was thinkin' of takin' her home, Billy. What do you think of that? Will you spring for her train ticket?"

Vail snorted and leaned back in his chair again. "Hell, I reckon. Tell Henry to hammer you out a pay voucher. When you figure on leaving?"

Longarm rose, donned his hat, and headed for the door. "How 'bout an hour ago?"

Chapter 5

Wheels clattered. The cattle car jerked back and forth on its old, squawky undercarriage.

There was the smell of cow shit and sage and straw and greasewood warming in the heat of the afternoon. Longarm, asleep with his head resting back against the rough wooden wall, was only half-aware of these sensations. But another one woke him—a yielding weight against his right thigh and a human warmth pressing against his fly and seeping into his loins, quickening his blood.

He opened his eyes and dropped his chin.

Arlis Pine's head with its tangle of auburn hair lay in his lap. She'd been sleeping beside him, her own head resting back against the cattle car wall like Longarm's own, and then as he slept he'd felt her head drift down to rest against his shoulder. The jostling of the train must have knocked it off his shoulder and onto his lap.

Her rich lips moved, and he could see her eyeballs

moving behind her softly closed, lightly tanned lids.
Dreaming. She gave a little grunt and moved her head
slightly, sort of grinding one cheek and jaw against Longarm's cock curled like a fat, slumbering snake inside his
summer-weight balbriggans and trying to mind its own
damn business.

Longarm winced at the not unpleasant sensation, having no desire for it here, stemming as it did from the caress of a girl who had only yesterday tried to ventilate
him. His cheeks warmed slightly with chagrin. Shit, he
felt blood oozing into the consarned member in question, and the dreaded, albeit slow, stiffening—a snake
roused by the smell of a nearby gopher.

The federal lawman set a hand on the girl's shoulder.
It was slender and warm. He thought about jostling her a
little to wake her, but embarrassment at his still-growing
member forestalled the movement. He felt the round
firmness of the girl's left breast pressing against his hand
that lay palm-down on the straw-strewn floor of the car
at his right side. The orb seemed to swell slightly—in
response to the hardening she must have been feeling in
her sleep, beneath her cheek?

"Arlis," Longarm said finally, having to clear his throat
first. This wasn't going to get any easier for him—in fact
the longer he delayed waking her, the more embarrass-
ing it was sure to become. "Uhh . . . Arlis . . ."

She sighed and smacked her lips. Vaguely, he noted
that her lips owned the shape one would call "bee-stung"
or, if one were of a more depraved nature, "blowjob"
lips, and as she parted them slightly, he could see the
whiteness of her upper and lower front teeth beneath
pink gums.

She made a little sucking sound as she squirmed some more, and groaned.

Feeling more and more desperate, Longarm gave his right leg a shake. "Miss Pine, wake up." He squeezed her shoulder.

She jerked her head a few inches off his lap with a start, looking around as though trying to remember where she was. Finally, her hazel gaze drifted to his scuffed cavalry boots extending straight out in front of her, his ankles crossed, before she turned her head up to see Longarm staring down at her.

She dropped her gaze to his lap—yep, she'd felt it, all right—and tucked her lower lip under her front teeth deliciously. She rose more quickly then, until her hair was snaking up and off his dusty tobacco-tweed trousers, and a flush darkened her cheeks as she smoothed the locks of her hair back away from her face.

"Sorry."

"That's all right," Longarm said, his ears warming as he heaved himself stiffly to his feet, the backs of his thighs cramping from the hard wooden floor. "Leg was fallin' asleep is all."

She rolled her eyes sideways to glance up at his crotch. He thought he saw a wicked little gleam in them. She smacked her lips. "Like I said—sorry. Fell right dead asleep. I reckon it was too cold to get much shuteye last night in Chugwater."

"Too bad there wasn't a regular combination headed out this way," he said, stretching to cover his body's automatic, albeit lecherous, lust at the caress of a young, pretty girl. He slid the cattle car's heavy wooden door open and was met with a heavy *whush!* of hot, dry air that it nearly toppled him backwards. Getting both boots under himself again, he stood in the four-foot opening, squinting out at the countryside.

The Burlington Northern combination they'd hopped at Denver's Union Station had carried them as far as Chugwater, Wyoming, north of Cheyenne, where they had a five-hour layover last night in the little unheated station house. There was a spur line from there to the little army outpost of Hope Springs, about sixty miles northwest of the old Bozeman Trail. But the spur line only hauled passengers out that way once every two weeks; otherwise, the three- or four-car combinations were made up solely of freight, including hogs and cattle.

Judging by the stench and remaining half-dried pies, cattle had been the last passengers in Longarm's and Miss Pine's car. At least they hadn't been hogs, the stench of which was too much like the musky aroma of an overfilled latrine. The spur line charged anyone who wanted to ride the less than rustic freight combinations half the usual passenger price, so the cost to Uncle Sam for this leg of Longarm and Arlis Pine's journey to Lightning Flat was a dollar and a half apiece.

The cost to Longarm's backside and shoulders that had been rubbing against the floor and wall of the stock car for the past six hours—the train only traveled about sixteen-miles an hour fully stoked and was forever stopping to take on water or for cattle on the tracks—was great indeed. He felt as though a bull from a railroad yard had pummeled him without surcease with a hard oak axe handle.

"Me—I don't much need the comforts of a dolled up Pullman sleeper car," Arlis said and yawned. She'd no doubt seen Longarm detrain from such a sleeper just yesterday morning. "But a regular coach would have been nice." She stood beside the lawman, turning to look past him up the tracks. "Look—there's Hope Springs. 'Bout time, if you ask me."

"My sentiments exactly," the federal lawman said, holding his hat brim while looking up along the five-car combination and past the black iron locomotive with its diamond stack spewing black smoke and glowing cinders.

Beyond, the humble little shacks that comprised a town of sorts—really just an old hide hunters' camp that was now mostly home to blanket Indians, stove-up outlaws, down-at-heel cavalrymen who garrisoned the fifteen- or twenty-man army outpost, whiskey peddlers, and whores—took shape among the low, rolling hills of sagebrush and greasewood. This was the end of the spur line, but Longarm intended to acquisition a couple of sturdy horses with which he and Arlis would complete their journey to Lightning Flat. He would pick up the trail of the killers of Alvin Pine there, and once he'd run them to ground, he'd return both his horse and Miss Pine's to the army quartermaster at Hope Springs.

That was the plan, anyway. But first he had to find the fort's commander and then the quartermaster. As it was getting on late in the afternoon, with the distant peaks of the Bighorns silhouetted against the western sky, he and Arlis would have to shelter in the camp for the night, then ride out first thing in the morning.

As the train chugged up to the plank-board, tar-paper shack that served as a train station out here, Longarm and Arlis grabbed their gear. Longarm leaped down from the cattle car while the car was still inching along, the tires squawking like nuns on a Friday night in Perdition. He set his saddle, saddlebags, and war sack down to extend a hand up toward Arlis. She waved him off with an air of disgust. Her ratty burlap war sack hanging down her back by a frayed rope, she leaped from the car and landed flatfooted in the pebbly dust beside it.

Longarm was getting miffed at the girl's haughty attitude. "In spite of what you must have cooked up about me in that mule head of yours, I did not kill your father. True, I promised to help protect him, and I failed miserably at that. But I did not kill him."

"Don't get your longhandles in a twist, lawdog." Arlis lifted her hat to run a slim hand through her sweat-damp hair while she scrutinized the rough-hewn hamlet beyond the station shack. "I've already decided I was wrong to come grease you that way. Truth to tell, I was expecting a whimpering, yellow-livered scoundrel. Never did expect you to hop the next train with me." She gave him a crooked look. "I reckon you're all right . . . for a federal."

Longarm felt his shoulders loosen pleasingly while a genuine smile quirked at his mustache. "Well, I do appreciate that, Miss Pine."

"Arlis."

"In that case, then, call me Longarm. Most folks do."

She let her ironic hazel gaze flicker down past the buckle of his cartridge belt to his crotch. "I reckon I found out why when I fell asleep in your lap."

His ears warming all over again, Longarm cleared his throat and gathered his gear, including his rifle, heaving it all onto his shoulders with a grunt. "Why don't you get a room at the hotel yonder." He jutted his chin at a three-story structure about fifty yards away. Large letters above the shake-shingled porch roof announced HOPE SPRINGS SALOON & HOTEL.

Unpainted, basted with tumbleweeds along its stone foundation, and leaning slightly to the southeast, the structure looked as though it could be toppled by the next strong wind blowing out of the Bighorns. Even so, it appeared to be the largest and best-kept dwelling in the dusty, smelly little jerkwater that appeared to be Hope Springs. "We'll spend the night here, head out first thing tomorrow. I'll fetch us a couple of cavalry remounts, have 'em all set to go."

The girl nodded, then, tossing the war sack down her back. She tipped her hat brim low and began tramping along a narrow trail through the sage toward the sun-blasted little town where only a few horses and men stirred among the bleached buildings. The dwellings all sat willy-nilly, mingling cozily with stock pens, corrals, hay barns, and privies. The military outpost was just right of the town, distinguishable by a timbered portal the cross beam of which read simply CAV. OUTPOST, HOPE SPRINGS, WYO. TERR.

Most of the buildings were made of mud brick and sod or sun-silvered cottonwood logs. There were only a half dozen, not including two large barns flanking the place with three-pole corrals and feed and storage sheds, and a windmill that grated raucously in the dry air that kicked up tiny tornadoes all about the hard-packed yard fronting the main offices and enlisted men's barracks.

As Longarm tramped beneath the portal's cross beam, his gear making his shoulders sweat-soggy, but not trusting to stow it anywhere far from his person, he saw a handful of soldiers lounging in the shade beneath brush arbors. One was strumming a guitar. Another was whittling a short stick into what looked like a duck. A big man with a paunch and wearing a forage cap with the leather bill torn off was teaching a slender yellow cur to sit up and howl for hardtack treats. The three men were sitting outside the crude, larger cabin to the right of a smaller one whose shingle announced POST HEADQUARTERS.

On the headquarters' timbered door another, smaller shingle hung askew from a rusty nail, the words CAPTAIN M. L. BUTLER burned into it.

Longarm stopped in what must have served as the post parade yard—he doubted it had seen anything resembling a military parade in the past ten years—and regarded the soldiers who regarded him with only vague interest despite the federal moon-and-star badge on his black frock coat's coal dust–streaked lapel.

"Hidy."

The soldiers said nothing. The guitar-picker kept picking but a little more softly and slowly than before. The cur looked over its shoulder at the lawman, its eyes as uninterested as those of the men.

Longarm glanced at the commanding officer's cabin. "The head honcho in?"

None of the soldiers said anything. The picker continued picking. He began singing softly while the other two men and the cur pointedly ignored the badge-sporting man in the frock coat and coffee-brown Stetson, as well. Longarm probably shouldn't have worn his badge to the outpost. Especially on these most remote garrisons there were bound to be men with paper on their heads, or who had tussled with the law in sundry ways before that had left them colicky at the sight of a dime's worth of tin and copper pinned to a coat.

The lawman shrugged and walked up to the humble post headquarters building, and knocked on the door. No answer. But the latch clicked open. After a quick investigation and finding nothing in the small office but an old steak bone swarming with flies on a tin plate on the office's sole, small desk, one broken leg of which was propped up by a Sears-Roebuck catalogue, he headed around back of the main post buildings to one of the two stock barns.

Here he found a lone soldier forking hay into a crib. He was little better tempered than the others, and the man did offer the information that he was a mere private and that he alone was in charge of the post stables since the quartermaster sergeant had been killed by a mule's kick two weeks ago. The private only shrugged when Longarm asked about the commanding officer. He didn't seem at all bothered by Longarm's request for two horses; he simply had the federal lawman fill out and sign a couple of "property request" forms and pick his mounts.

Longarm was none too impressed by the holding corral, but for himself he chose a dapple-gray gelding with straight legs and a star on its snout and which seemed otherwise to have been well fed and watered, giving it some bottom to possibly carry the lawman on a long run through rough country. For Arlis he chose an army bay with light zebra spotting across its back and down its sides and which seemed to want to stay close to the dapple-gray. It, too, looked fit enough, and clear-eyed.

Longarm outfitted the bay with a Texas-styled saddle that was sitting over a stall partition gathering dust and which the private said had belonged to an old owlhoot who'd ridden into the post dead one day, lung-shot. The post soldiers had kept the Texas stock saddle, as they had nothing else to do with it, though of course cavalry riders were required to use the McClellans.

Both horses rigged, Longarm mounted the dapple-gray, pinched his hat brim to the private, and gigged the gray on out the entrance portal, jerking the zebra-striped bay along behind him. He followed a powdery trail twisting through the sage. He'd no sooner ridden into the town of Hope Springs only sixty yards away than he spied a soldier with his yellow-striped trousers down, bending a naked, copper-skinned Indian girl backward across a rain barrel outside a mercantile building.

The girl was digging her heels into the man's back as he hammered away between her legs, laughing. An uncorked whiskey bottle stood at his wide-spread feet.

Yep, this was one hell of a backwater Perdition, all right. Seems times never changed this far off the beaten path . . .

Longarm had just turned his head away from the public display of craven carnality when the unmistakable voice of Arlis Pine peeled like a gut-shot coyote's wail over the town's sun-scorched roofs.

Longarm's heart thudded and deep lines dug across his forehead as he tried to get his bearings.

The dead marshal's daughter was screaming bloody murder.

Chapter 6

The girl's scream rose again. It was followed by a man's yelp.

Longarm rammed his heels into the gray's flanks and followed the sounds of combat straight up the broad main street of Hope Springs and then around to the front of the Hope Springs Saloon and Hotel. He reined the gray to a halt just as a man in a long leather coat and grimy checked trousers staggered onto the gallery through the batwing doors. Clutching his crotch with both hands, the man stopped in front of the shuddering doors, lifted his head, and bellowed.

He staggered forward, continuing to clutch his crotch, from which an ebony-handled knife protruded, blood welling up around the fancy pig-sticker to stain the man's pants. He staggered down the three porch steps and stumbled into the street, where he dropped about ten feet in front of Longarm, wailing, "The little bitch! Oh, the infernal little frickin' bitch done tried to cut my balls off!" He sobbed, throwing his head back and stretching the rope-like chords in his scrawny, leathery neck. "Oh, *gawwd*, it hurts!"

Longarm dropped the reins of the bay gelding he was leading as he fairly leaped from the saddle to hit the ground running. Inside the saloon, the girl continued to scream and curse while several men were shouting angrily.

Crack!

The pistol shot from inside the saloon sounded like a branch banged against an empty rain barrel. A man screamed and yowled.

Crack!

The second shot peeled as Longarm bounced up the three porch steps in one long stride. Over the batwings he saw a man in cavalry blues stumble toward him backwards, away from a commotion in the rear of the dingy place, before sprawling across a table as though dropped from the sky. His arms and legs dangled toward the hard-packed earthen floor, head hanging down the side of the table nearest Longarm, gray eyes flickering as they stared up at the lawman as if in silent beseeching.

A neat round hole in his right cheek oozed liver-colored blood down into his left eye.

Back in the shadows at the rear of the place, a man grunted, "Hold her, damnit! Hold her still, for chrissakes!"

"No!" Arlis Pine raged, and as Longarm's eyes quickly adjusted to the oily shadows threaded with tobacco smoke, he saw a tall man in a tan hat and also wearing cavalry blues try to wrestle Arlis's smoking .36 Smith & Wesson from her clenched right fist.

Two other men—one in a grungy uniform, one in ratty civilian attire—were holding her awkwardly a couple feet above the floor, the soldier with an arm snaked around her thighs. The civilian held her around the neck and shoulders while she twisted and writhed, trying to kick at a third man, who grappled for her gun.

"Let me go, you fairy cocksuckers, or so help me . . . !"

Her voice choked off as the tallest of the three, wearing a captain's bar on the shoulder of his blue wool tunic, barked a curse and jerked the weapon free of Arlis's hand at last. As he gritted his teeth and leaned forward, drawing his hand holding the girl's gun back as though to ram it across her face, Longarm drew his Colt double-action .44/40 and rocked the hammer back.

The ratcheting sounded inordinately loud in the low-ceilinged room, and it stopped the captain's fist about halfway from its mark.

"The girl's with me."

The captain swung around, eyes like two blue coals in the shadows. He had a hawkish face with a scar twisting the right side of his upper lip, enhancing his savage countenance. A wing of coal-black hair hung like a raven's across his left eye. He wore his tunic over a ratty red underwear shirt.

"Who're you?" The man's eyes flicked toward the badge on Longarm's lapel, as did those of the two other men, who stood frozen but still holding Arlis above the floor. The captain stared down the length of her upraised body at Longarm standing with gun raised just inside the batwings.

"Lawman," grunted the beefy, shaggy-headed corporal holding Arlis.

"Let her down easy," Longarm ordered.

He spied movement toward his right and rolled his eyes to see a thin man with a broad, pitted nose raise his head above the bar, eyes wide with caution. The bartender, most likely, who'd ducked down behind his bar when the lead started flying.

The captain stretched his lips in a smile that didn't reach his eyes. It didn't even make it to his nose. "What's she to you? Can we pay you for her?"

"Let her down easy, Captain. I'm not going to ask you again."

The captain's smile broadened—if you could call it a smile. He turned full around to face Longarm, the girl's .36 in his left hand but the barrel aimed at the floor. "Girls are few and far between in these parts. Young ones that ain't been . . . shall we say, *corrupted*?"

Longarm stared at the captain, his face rigid as granite, his own eyes focused as sharp as two chips of freshly forged steel.

The captain sighed in defeat, shrugging slightly. He glanced over his left shoulder at the men behind him. "All right, fellas. You heard the man. Let her—"

He clipped off the sentence as he jerked his head back toward Longarm, snaking his right hand across his waist for the Colt Army holstered in the cross-draw position on his left hip. At the same time, the other two men suddenly released Arlis, and she hit the floor with a scream, just as the captain's Colt came up in a blur of cunning, practiced, quick-draw motion.

He was quick. But he wasn't quick enough to beat a man who already had his own gun drawn and cocked.

Longarm triggered his .44 twice, the explosions making the entire room jump and causing the barman to drop quickly down behind the rough-hewn bar. The captain screamed, stretching his scarred upper lip back from his teeth that shone white in the shadows, as he stumbled straight back toward the stairs.

The other men, now unencumbered by Arlis's flailing flesh, ripped hands toward the hoglegs on their hips. Neither got a gun even half out of its sheath before the lawman's .44 exploded two more times, sending the soldier dancing back toward the stairs and the civilian spinning and flying over a table near the newel post.

Longarm squinted through the powder smoke wafting before him, shuttling his gaze from the man piled up at the bottom of the stairs, making a weird whistling sound with his lips, and the civilian who'd fallen over the table to the soldier's left.

The civilian didn't seem to be moving, but Longarm, accustomed to such dustups, was cautious. Arlis was on her back on the floor, groaning and writhing from side to side while holding her head in her hands. The barman had again dared a peek above the edge of his plankboard bar, showing only two close-set, fear-wide eyes and a pale forehead capped with dark brown hair oiled and crookedly parted.

"Stay where you are, mister," Longarm told the barman, not knowing what, if any, the barman's slice of this was. Out here, a man trusted no one. Especially a lawman.

"I'm stayin' right here," the barman muttered, ducking his head once more.

Longarm walked forward. As he did, Arlis rose up on

her elbows, looking around bewilderedly. She looked all right, just daze and frightened.

"Stay there," Longarm ordered the girl as he stepped around her, inspecting the soldier at the bottom of the stairs. He lay on his side, blood and white brain matter dribbling out from the hole in his right temple. He wasn't moving.

Longarm had just begun to turn toward where he'd dropped the civilian, when the man's head appeared suddenly from behind the table he'd fallen over. He was bald on top, with lice-flecked hair hanging down over his ears. He had a bright, enraged gleam in both his eyes as he stretched a cocked Remington across the table at Longarm.

Again, Longarm was faster, pivoting on his hips and crouching as he drilled two holes through the center of the man's forehead, spaced not two inches apart. The Remington barked, stabbing smoke and flames, the bullet warming the air beside Longarm and shattering a glass on a shelf behind the bar.

The man's lower jaw dropped and he said, "Ugh!" as his eyes instantly dimmed and he fell back behind the table in a loose-jointed heap.

Hearing a groan behind him, the lawman wheeled, extending the .44 from his right hip. Behind the bar, the barman jerked back with a start, a horrified look on his ugly, craggy face with its long, bulbous nose and close-set eyes, holding his hands shoulder-high, palms out, fingers tight together.

"Don't shoot, damnit," he squealed. "Don't shoot me—I don't want no trouble. Hell, I own the place!"

Longarm waved his smoking, empty .44, hoping the

barman hadn't been counting his shots, and growled, "Come on out of there, friend. And keep them hands raised."

The man stepped sideways quickly, stumbling, as he came out from behind the bar and stood near the batwings, hands raised high above his head as he glanced at the dead man sprawled on the table by the door. "Well, the little miss sure drilled Kinch—that's for sure."

"Who's the captain?"

"Butler. From the post over yonder." The barman had pitched his voice with distaste, wrinkling his nose. "Sour devil. I ain't sorry to see him dead, and I ain't sayin' that 'cause you're the one still standin'."

Longarm kicked the captain onto his back. He'd drilled the man twice through the chest, and he'd been dead before he'd hit the floor beside a four-by-four ceiling joist from which a lariat and a dusty hurricane lamp hung. The half-open eyes stared up at Longarm from beneath the wing of coal-black hair. The scarred lip was curled in voiceless misery.

"Uh-uh. That there is Harry 'The Hatchet' Milbank from southern New Mexico Territory. Wondered what ever happened to him." Longarm chuffed and shook his head as he stared down at the dead man, while his hands automatically shook the spent cartridges from his .44 and quickly replaced them with fresh ammo from his shell belt. "Went an' joined the army, finagled himself a commission and an assignment at one of the remotest outposts he could find."

"In the two years he's been here, him an' his men ran all the good women out of town. Them that weren't dead packed up and left a long time ago."

"What else did he have going out here?"

The barman, who'd lowered his hands to his shoulders and curled his fingers toward his palms, glanced down warily at the dead outlaw turned army captain, as though wanting to make sure the man was truly deceased. "Rumor had it he was runnin' whiskey and rifles to the Injuns up north, and robbing the U.P. Flier every few months."

"No law in town, huh?"

"He was it."

Longarm glanced at the dead civilian on the other side of the back table. "Who's he?"

"Post sutler. Name's Chapel."

"Figures."

"They was playin' cards when Little Miss come in," the barman said, glancing at Arlis still on the floor and now tucking her head between her upraised knees. "Grabbed her damn near right away. There wasn't nothin' I could've done. Shit, them fellas is . . . was . . . polecats of the baddest stripe I ever seen." He spat in disgust. "I'm glad they're dead. Just hope the army don't send us more just like 'em or worse."

Longarm asked the barman his name, and the man lowered his hands as he said, "Emil Lawton."

"Well, haul that wolfbait on outta here, Mr. Lawton." Longarm holstered his Colt and drew the keeper thong across its hammer. He reached down and pulled the girl up by one arm, folding her gently over his right shoulder as he turned toward the stairs. "Me and Little Miss are gonna take a couple of your rooms."

Lawton nodded. "The doors ain't locked."

"I'll fetch the keys later. When you're done hauling

your customers out to a nice, deep ravine, heat some bathwater for Little Miss. She'll take it in her room."

Leaving the barman looking over the dead men skeptically, Longarm headed on up the creaky stairs. The girl groaned and weakly cursed her attackers a few times, gradually regaining her wits.

"Bastards," she muttered tightly.

Longarm passed the second-floor landing and continued on up to the third story, as it seemed the higher up one went in a frontier hotel, the better and quieter the rooms. After a hasty inspection of the third-floor hall, which was padded with a sour-smelling red carpet runner, he came to a door identified by a crude wooden plaque as the PRESIDENTIAL SUITE. He opened the door and dropped the girl onto a bed with a musty-smelling, lace-edged, red velvet canopy that hadn't had the dust pounded out of it in years.

Longarm gentled the girl's head onto a poplin-covered pillow and began to straighten. Her eyes regained their focus and acquired a haunted cast as she grabbed his coat lapels, pulling him toward her as she cried, "Please don't go, Longarm! I'm *awful* frightened. Oh, please stay with me! I'll make it worth your time—I swear I will!"

Chapter 7

"Ah, now, Miss Arlis," Longarm said in a faintly chastising tone, gently peeling the girl's hands from his coat lapels. "You're just a little overwrought. It's to be expected after all you've been through so recent-like."

"Please," she said in a beseeching, little girl's tone, propping herself on her elbows. "I'm really not as tough as I let on sometimes."

"Could've fooled me after our little shindig at Union Station."

"I'm temperamental—right enough. Just born hot-blooded, I reckon. It works the other way, too. I get awful frightened, bein' out here all alone now, with Pa gone an' all." She rolled innocent eyes up at him from beneath her thin brows, her hair falling down her shoulders attractively and framing her tan, heart-shaped face. "I'd really like you to stay with me for a while. Like I said, I'll make it worth your time. I know how men are."

Longarm straightened and couldn't help feeling the

old male pull in his loins as she drew her knees together and bent her legs to one side, sagging down on the bed beneath him—a hot little vixen if he'd ever seen one. This was a surprising change. He hadn't figured her for the coquette. But she might have been playing him straight up and really did just want his company after she'd come so close to being gang-banged and likely getting her throat cut to boot.

"Well, you're wrong about this feller. I'd stay with you for free, Miss Arlis. But I scrounged us up a couple of cayuses from the cavalry post, and I'm gonna have to find a feed barn for 'em close by."

Longarm dragged his gaze from the girl, whose breasts had seemed to grow and swell against her checkerboard wool shirt as she stared up at him all scared and wanton-like. He walked over to the window, which faced a dusty lot covered in sagebrush and greasewood. There was a privy back there, and an old prairie schooner resting on its axles and grown up with buck brush and yucca.

He opened the window to let some air into the musty "suite." The only thing suite-like about it was the slightly larger than normal, canopied bed and a fancy mahogany dresser that was scarred and scraped and boasted a cracked, warped, fly-specked mirror. Turning to the girl, he said, "There—some air oughta help your condition. How's your head?"

"I'm coming around, I reckon. Those four varmints meant to rape me, didn't they?"

"I reckon they weren't tryin' to haul you up here for a Sunday school lesson. You're all right now, and I have a feelin' the hombre on the street won't be hassling no more girls never." Longarm gave her a crooked frown.

"Where'd that ivory-gripped shoat-poker come from, anyway?"

"Had it sheathed down my back, under my shirt collar. Figured it might come in handy."

"I'll be damned—you did have a hideout."

Arlis rose up on one elbow, pinning him again with those suddenly seductive hazel eyes, and raised her mouth corners. "A girl's gotta have a few secrets, Longarm." She wriggled around some more, grinding her boots together, catlike.

"I got a feelin' you have more secrets than I could ever fathom."

"I'm older than you think."

"I haven't thought about it." Longarm walked to the door.

"If you did think about it," the girl asked him, her voice a raspy purr, "how old would you say I was?"

Longarm frowned at her, not liking the turn of the conversation. He was too damn busy to be pestered like this. He was beginning to think he'd liked her better when she was trying to punch .36-caliber windows through him. In spite of himself, he shrugged. "I don't know—fifteen, maybe."

He opened the door but drew it only partway open as she said, "I'm twenty."

Longarm shuttled his skeptical gaze back to the bed, where she was regarding him, cheek resting on the heel of a hand, with that annoying, mocking gaze, twin mounds of her breasts rising and falling heavily behind her shirt. Some color had been added to her cheeks.

"I know I don't look it," Arlis said. "I have a naturally young look, and with all these loose clothes you can't see my figure. But I'm damn near all filled out . . . and I might let you take a peek if you stayed here with me and let someone else tend our horses. I could get accosted again while you're gone." She jerked her chin at the open window, along the sides of which dusty curtains the same color as the bed canopy danced in the warm, dry breeze. "Who knows what's skulkin' around out there?"

"I just had a look out there, Miss Arlis." Longarm felt his ears warm with automatic lust. Twenty? He'd be damned if he wasn't starting to believe her, while at the same time wanting no part of her. "Nothing but sand and sagebrush. You'll be fine."

He pulled the door open farther and started to go out but stopped once more as she said, "Longarm?"

He sighed. "Yep?"

She moved her curved body again like a snake testing the temperature in its hole. "Will you fetch my pig-sticker for me? I'd feel a whole lot safer with it back in its sheath."

Longarm gave a wry chuff as he pulled his eyes off of her and those enticing twin mounds beneath her shirt. He stomped into the hall and closed the door quickly behind him, as though locking a rabid bobcat in its cage.

He hustled downstairs, where Lawton was dragging the captain across the floor toward the batwings, the barman's wrists hooked under the outlaw-soldier's armpits. Harry "The Hatchet" Milbank's eyes were still open and staring forlornly at his own bloody undershirt as Lawton hauled him toward the doors. That wing of black hair flapped over the outlaw's left eye.

The man who'd been stretched across the table with one of Arlis's .36 slugs through his cheek, was gone.

Only a small pool of fresh blood remained on the floor near the far end of the table.

"You could give me a hand," Lawton snarled, glaring at Longarm as he pushed backwards out the batwings and into the glaring sunlight.

"You let 'em in," Longarm said, following the barman and the dead man outside. "You can haul 'em out."

He stopped on the gallery. Squinting against the westering sun and digging into his shirt pocket for a three-for-a-nickel cheroot, he regarded the man whom Arlis had all but emasculated with her ivory-handled Arkansas toothpick. The man lay slumped forward on his knees, boot toes poking into the finely ground dust and horse-shit of the street.

"Hey, who's this fella?" Longarm asked the barman as he scratched a match to life on a thumbnail and touch the feeble flame to his cigar.

The barman, who was dragging Harry the Hatchet westward along the broad main drag and was now being followed with interest by a shaggy, bur-laden collie dog, stopped and squinted one incredulous eye at the lawman. "They called him Stiles," he said with an impatient air. Then he continued dragging his carrion toward a ravine snaking along the far edge of the town and marked by a scraggly line of cottonwoods and willows.

The collie followed, head down, sniffing at the dead man's boots.

Longarm sucked the cigar smoke deep into his lungs, enjoying the burn. It was a nice distraction from the coppery stench of spilled blood and the girl lounging on the canopied bed up yonder. He could do without her. Too much freight involved there, not the least of which was the fact he'd let her and her old man down after he'd promised to protect Alvin Pine from Del Sager.

He took another deep drag on the cigar and looked again at the barman angling toward the south side of the street, Harry the Hatchet's spurred boot heals carving twin troughs in the dust behind him. "Hey, there a feed barn in town, where I can stow my cayuses overnight?"

Again, the barman stopped and gave him a testy look. After nearly half a minute, he canted his head toward his left shoulder and said, "Vincent's Federated. Just over yonder." He canted his head toward his other shoulder, and slitted his eyes. "No offense, but how long you gonna be stayin' with us here in Hope Springs, anyways?"

"Don't worry, Lawton."

Smoking, Longarm dropped down the gallery's steps and kicked the man called Stiles onto his back. Stiles was dead, eyes rolled up beneath his dark-red brows. His lips were peeled back, revealing small, square teeth yellow as dried corn. The lawman jerked the knife out of the man's bloody crotch. It made a wet, scrunching sound. He swiped the blade across the dead man's shoulder several times to clean it.

Around the cigar in his teeth, Longarm said, "I ain't plannin' on sinkin' a taproot hereabouts. I reckon hope springs eternal, but that's just too damn long for me."

Longarm flipped the knife in the air, caught it by its handle, and grinned at Lawton. The barman shook his head and continued dragging Harry the Hatchet off toward the ravine. The collie followed, mewling hungrily.

Longarm took the horses over to Vincent's Federated Feed and Livery Barn, gave them a little closer going over as well as a grooming, making sure all eights were sound and well shod. He left the horses in the care of a freckle-faced boy who couldn't have been much over eleven years old but whose face was already as craggy as an old man's—he had the look of hard work and little mercy about him, as did everyone who lived out here— and headed back to the half-deserted little town, toward the Hope Springs Saloon.

A western mesa was spearing the bright yellow sun, and the shadows cast by the salmon-dappled sage and rabbit brush were several yards long. Tramping along an especially forlorn section of town, Longarm spied a scrawny coyote panting down a narrow gully that cut through a corner of the quiet little burg. Probably heading for its favorite trash pile or chicken coop. Longarm heard pigs snorting in a pen as he passed a log barn and tar-paper shack. A stout, apron-clad woman was speaking German as she tossed slop to the hogs over a pine-board rail.

As he pushed through the batwings of the Hope Springs Saloon, Longarm saw Lawton hauling a wooden bucket of steaming water up the stairs at the far end of the main hall. All that remained of the dead men was sawdust-sprinkled bloodstains on the floor.

Longarm asked the man if he had any Maryland rye laying around too lonely for words, and the barman only stopped and turned to him with a pained look, planting a broad hand on the rail beside him and saying, "Rye from where?"

"Never mind. Mind if I help myself?"

"Never met a trustworthy lawdog, but since I ain't overrun with help around here and your Little Miss sure likes her bathwater hot, go ahead."

As the man continued on up to the third floor with his bucket of water, Longarm rummaged around behind the bar. He found a bottle of rye that he thought he could stomach, then poured himself several fingers in a water glass. He hauled the drink over to a table and eased down into a chair with his back to the wall and a good view of both the front door and the rear stairs. He relit the cheroot he'd only smoked half of earlier, took a deep drag, blew it at the low, smoke-stained rafters, and followed it up with a liberal sip of the rye. The busthead wasn't from Maryland, but it cut the blood stench and trail dust well enough, and, surprisingly, it complemented the faint bourbon-and-juniper taste of his cheap cigar.

Lawton came down looking haggard and moving shamble-footed. He dropped the still-steaming bucket at the end of the bar and sighed as he made his way behind it.

"The girl comfortable?" Longarm asked the man.

"Hell, she's in the Presidential Suite, ain't she?"

"Very finely appointed room, too. You must have been a hotelier in St. Louis."

"I know sarcasm when I hear it," the man said, still a trifle breathless from his labors as he reached under the bar for a bottle. "I do the best I can. And it wasn't my fault what happened, neither." He muttered a curse as he popped the cork on the bottle, splashed bourbon into a shot glass, and threw half the shot back. He looked at Longarm. "What're you and her doin' out here, anyways? I take it she ain't your prisoner."

"She's the daughter of Alvin Pine."

Lawton nodded, looked down at the rest of his shot,

then polished it off, tipping his head back. He splashed more bourbon into the glass. "I heard about that. You after Sager?"

"That's right. Heard he was headed into the Bear Lodge Mountains." Longarm took another sip of his drink, then with the heel of his hand smashed a spider scuttling across his table.

"Too bad you didn't get here day before yesterday. You mighta run right into his brother, Little Louis. Came through here, spent the night with a Mex whore he's been ridin' with, then headed out first thing the next mornin'. Got drunk and was braggin' about how he was off to meet his older brother at one of their most secret hideouts in all their stompin' grounds. Said they was gonna get their gang back together and get back to what they was doin' before . . ."

Lawton let his words die like an evening breeze when he saw Longarm scowling at him from the far side of the room, from beneath shaggy auburn brows, the ridges of his sun-seared cheeks knotted like muscles.

"Somethin' I said?"

"Sager's brother was through here?"

"That's right." Lawton nodded and turned his glass between his thumb and index finger. "Little Louis, they call him. Apparently their father was Big Louis. Big Louis Sa—"

"And he said he was off to meet his brother in the Bear Lodge Mountains?"

"That's what he said. You missed him two days back. The tracks of him and his boys are probably long gone by now. We had one helluva dust storm here yesterday, then rain last night. If you're trackin' Sager, you best

head up around Pancho Butte. Heard tell he's got a
hideout in one o' them canyons back in there. Likely,
you'll never find it. And I'll tell you straight, you don't
want to find it, Mr. Lawman sir."

Longarm stared at the man, his blood quickening. He
threw back the shot, then wiped the dead spider from the
heel of his hand onto his tobacco-tweed slacks, his
brows ridged thoughtfully. He'd thought he would have
to wait until he got to Lightning Flat to pick up Sager's
trail. But that one was likely far colder even than the
one his little brother had left from right here in Hope
Springs.

Lawton must have been reading Longarm's mind.
"Like I said, Little Louis's trail is probably colder'n a
witch's tit." A little fear came into his voice, and he
spoke more quickly. "You best go on up to Lightning
Flat. This is the long way around the Bear Lodge Mountain country. Rugged country north of here. Louis probably knows a shortcut."

"Or maybe he's meeting his brother not far from
here." Longarm was now speaking to his half-empty
glass of rye. "Maybe they have 'em a hideout on the
southern end of the Bear Lodge Mountains, and that's
where Sager's meeting his kin." He narrowed an eye as
he looked up at Lawton. "Little Louis, you say? That
wouldn't be Little Louis Estevez, would it?"

Lawton swallowed anxiously, and furled his own
brows as he nodded reluctantly. "That's right. When him
and his brother started ridin' the owlhoot trail, Louis
took his ma's maiden name. So they could distinguish
themselves, I reckon."

Longarm chuckled mirthlessly, and threw back the

last of his drink. "Little Louis Estevez. Well, I'll be damned." He'd had no idea Estevez and Sager were related, much less brothers . . .

"What is it?"

"Little Louis's wanted for murder back in Cheyenne. Killed three stock detectives and a Pinkerton agent from over near the Rawhide Range when he was ridin' rough-shod for an outlaw rancher. Killin' nesters for twenty dollars a head. That was nigh on five years ago now."

Longarm was grinning down at his drink, his cheeks turning brassy, his eyes bright with expectation.

"Ah, shit," Lawton said, scowling across the bar at his sole patron. "You don't mention where you heard about Louis bein' here in Hope Springs, now, y'hear? Don't you mention me, goddamnit! Some say Louis's three times the polecat his older brother is, and I don't want him comin' back here and cuttin' my tongue out. Ah, shit! Ah, hell!" The barman punched the bartop with the heel of his right fist. "What'd I have to go and open my big mouth for, anyways?"

Chapter 8

When Longarm finished his drink, and thinking over his sudden change of plans, he headed upstairs for a nap.

He'd fetch Arlis in an hour or so, and he'd escort her over to a little Mexican café he'd passed on his way back from the livery barn. Then he'd take a whore's bath and retire, get an early start in the morning, into the southern reaches of the Bear Lodge Mountains, on the trail of Little Louis Estevez and his rancid-hided older brother, Del Sager.

If he could take both killers down together, all the better.

He tramped down the third-floor hall under the weight of all his gear except his saddle, which he'd left at the livery barn, stopped at the door of the room next to Arlis's, and set his hand on the knob.

"Longarm?" The girl's muffled voice had carried from behind her own door.

Longarm kept his hand on his doorknob but did not turn it. "Yeah?"

"Would you do me a favor?"

Longarm sighed and tramped on over to the door of the Presidential Suite. "What?"

"Would you scrub my back for me, please?"

Longarm chuckled. "Ha. Forget it, kid."

"Please?"

Longarm turned away from her door, and stopped. He frowned as he found himself considering the girl's request. Learning about the possibility of cutting brother Louis's trail right here in Hope Springs, and following the little miscreant right into Sager's lair, had lightened Longarm's mood considerably.

And somehow it had also made him more susceptible to the charms of one Miss Arlis Pine, whose twin mounds behind her well-filled checkerboard shirt were still indelibly imprinted on his incorrigible brain. She'd said she was twenty, and she certainly didn't act a day under thirty. What the hell—scrubbing the poor, orphaned young lady's back wouldn't come anywhere near the worst of his sins.

"The door unlocked?"

"Yes."

"Well, that was smart. Just invitin' more trouble . . ."

Longarm let his voice trail off as he swung the door open and saw the little brunette sitting in a tub in the middle of the room. She had her back to him, leaning forward with her arms around her upraised knees. It wasn't much of a tub—just a corrugated tin cylinder like the kind used for washing clothes in. It didn't cover much of her at all.

He felt as though a dull, icy spike had been driven up through his crotch, from the base of his balls and into his bladder. It made his knees tremble like those of a virgin bride.

She turned to look at him over her shoulder, the damp curls of her hair sliding across her narrow back that was silky smooth and pale as cream. Her spine curved delicately. Under one arm he could see the curve of a firm, round breast. Her eyes were watching his, and her lips spread a smile. She lifted one arm, exposing more of the curve of her right breast, and held up a soapy sponge.

Her hazel eyes glinted. "Thank you."

Longarm only grunted through a pinched windpipe and took the sponge out of the girl's hand. She turned her head forward to rest her chin on her knees, then swept a hand back to lift her hair up atop her head, giving him an open expanse of her slender, curving back to scrub. He gave another grunt and dropped to one knee, scowling despite the warm blood coursing through him, fanning a fire in his cheeks and setting up a faint tolling in his ears. He ran the sponge from her left shoulder blade to the right one, making small circular motions as he scrubbed.

The perfection of her back was marred only by a faint blemish along the right side of her spine about a third of the way down from her neck, and a pinpoint-sized mole just above her left hip. Longarm let his gaze caress the mole and was visited by the sneaky urge to kiss it.

Continuing to hold her hair up with one hand, Arlis frowned over her shoulder at him, turning just enough that he could see the entire side of her right breast and the tender pink, rosebud nipple. "A little harder, please?"

Longarm felt as though he'd swallowed a large spoon-
ful of molasses. He had to clear his throat before he
could say, "Harder . . . ?"

Her soft, pink lips spread another little smile. "With
the sponge—could you scrub a little harder?"

"Christ, what do I look like—your Chinese maid?"

She turned her head forward and groaned as he
pressed the sponge harder against her tender flesh, working up a lather and lifting a rosy pinkness all across her
back. She turned back to him once more, to say, "Are
you okay, Longarm? You look a little flushed."

"I ain't flushed."

"You can open another window, if you want."

"That's all right."

He dipped the sponge into the soapy water, his eyes
sliding down the curve of her spine and into the crack
between her buttocks. Steam wafted up before him. He
pressed the sponge against her once more, and made
larger circular motions against the middle of her back.

"Ohhh," she cooed. "That feels good."

After a time, she said softly, "Longarm?"

"Mhmmm?"

"Do you have a hard-on?"

He frowned at the back of her head, at her hand with
its fistful of damp hair, while he continued pressing the
sponge against her back, feeling the flames in his cheeks
flare up with gusto. "What?"

"Like the one in the stock car? When I woke up with
my head in your lap, I could feel it throbbing against my
cheek."

Longarm swallowed. Annoyance pricked him amid
the lust heat he found himself nearly overwhelmed by.

"You wanna sit here and gab all day, or you gonna let me scrub your back?"

"I think it's probably pretty clean by now."

The fires within him danced. "Right." He dropped the sponge in the water and stood, wincing as his tobacco-tweed trousers drew painfully taut against what he suddenly realized was a raging hard-on.

"Hold on."

"What now?" he grunted, lifting a furtive hand to pinch his fly away from his crotch to give his cock some room to breathe.

Suddenly, she rose up out of the water and turned toward him, then dropped back down in the tub, kneeling before him so that her face was only inches from his crotch. He could feel the heat of her gaze on his throbbing shaft, and then he could also feel her hands on his cartridge belt, unbuckling it until the shell belt and holster dropped to the floor at his mule-eared boots. A veil had dropped down over his eyes, so that he didn't see the maneuver until his belt was gone, and then she was expertly working on the one that held up his pants. Before he could respond or move his hands to brush hers away—if he'd wanted to, that was—she had his pants open and was reaching inside the fly of his balbriggans.

She giggled throatily as one hand gently cupped his balls while the other closed around his cock and slid slowly up from its base to the head. She smiled, keeping her lips together. Then they opened in the middle, and she nibbled her lower lip with her white upper front teeth. Her eyes rose to his, staring up at him coyly from beneath her thin brows a shade lighter than her hair.

"Now, that there is a cock," she whispered, letting her

lips swell as she spoke. They were red now, and wet.

Continuing to cup his balls with one hand, she gently
pulled his cock out of his fly. Her eyes widened when
she saw it, and her throat and lips moved as she swallowed. His shaft stood nearly straight up, the large mushroom head nodding slightly with every beat of his fully
stoked heart. She stared at the engorged appendage in
wide-eyed appreciation, eyes slightly crossed, then slowly
slid her hand up from its base before closing her fingers slowly around the nodding purple head.

"Oh, Jesus," she said. "Goddamn." She turned her head
sideways to look up the side of the organ, releasing his
balls now to run two fingers of her other hand up the side
of it, whispering, "You're hung like a fuckin' mule."

Longarm grated, wincing, "Such . . . farm talk . . . Miss
Pine . . ."

She giggled again down deep in her throat, eyes
glinting devilishly. Her breasts, sloping toward the tub,
swelled. The rosebud nipples hardened and jutted. She
lowered her hand to the ridge running around the head
of his cock. Staring up at him from beneath her brows,
she slid her tongue out from between her lips and touched
it ever so gently to the tip of the swollen head.

Longarm felt his legs tighten. He cursed under his
breath.

She smiled, staring up at him. As she opened her mouth
and slipped her lips over the purple head, she lowered
her eyes and swallowed him. Using her lips and hands,
and proving far more expert at fellatio than he ever would
have expected in a girl who looked so darn backwoods
innocent—at least in the ways of carnal knowledge—she
sucked him dry and swallowed every drop before cleaning

up the last remnants on his dwindling cock with her tongue.

"I suppose you're finished with me now," she said and pouted, canting her head to one side and tucking his drooping member into the hollow between her breasts, as though it were hers now.

She'd done too fine a job for him to just tug his pants up and leave. Instead, he pulled her up by her arms, until she stood before him, and kissed her long and deep, entwining her tongue with his own. He fondled her breasts—she had two good, round, firm handfuls—as she continued to play with his organ nestled against her soft, flat belly. It didn't take long for the single-minded member to come around once more, for another round with the delectable little damsel standing shin-deep in a tin tub before him.

When he was ready for her, he shucked quickly out of his clothes until he was as naked as she was, then picked her up in his arms and carried her over to the bed. He gentled her down on her butt then turned her around so that she faced the far wall. She gave a little giggle and dropped to her belly, tucking her legs beneath her and poking her round, little rump in the air.

She waggled it at him enticingly and shook her hair back across one shoulder as she looked at him across the other one, tugging pensively at her bottom lip with two fingers and narrowing one eye at his cock, with which he was slowly bearing down on her, setting his feet on the floor beside the bed.

"I think this is the only way that big ole dong's gonna fit in my little pussy, Longarm."

She gave her ass another little waggle. Grinning, she

swung her head forward and flung her arms out across
the bed above her shoulders in supplication.

He slid his shaft up inside her hot, sopping snatch,
and hammered away at the girl until, twenty minutes
later and after having nearly rammed the bed through
the opposite wall, they climaxed together and passed out,
limbs entangled.

Chapter 9

Longarm took his nap in Arlis's bed; then, waking a half hour later, he swatted her bare ass to rouse her from a deep slumber, and they headed off together in the search of the Chinese café and a bellyful of much-needed food. The saloon was quiet when they got back, only a couple of soldiers and two down-at-heel saddle tramps playing desultory games of low-stakes poker. Longarm bought a bottle and followed Arlis upstairs, but stopped at the door to his own room while she went on to hers, glancing incredulously over her shoulder.

"All played out?" she said with a devilish glint in her eyes.

"Yeah, I'm tuckered. A girl like you'd be the death of me."

"I doubt that." Arlis sighed. "Well, okay—I reckon we'll be up and on the trail early."

Longarm unlocked his door but did not go inside. "Arlis, you can sleep in tomorrow, if you like. Take your time getting on back to the Cross Fire. I'll be heading north."

She'd twisted her key in her own lock and now looked at him, incredulous. "I don't get it, Longarm. I thought you were gonna ride on back to Lightning Flat, pick up Del Sager's trail from there."

He'd delayed telling the girl of his new plan, because he knew, knowing how she was, that she'd want to be part of it. "I learned something from Lawton earlier. Sager's younger brother pulled through here two days ago, and headed north. Said he was on his way to meet his brother. I'm gonna head in the same direction in hopes of catchin' up to him. He has paper on his head, too. He might be younger than his older brother, but he's every bit the badman Sager is."

"When'd you learn all this?"

"This afternoon."

"Well, when the hell were you gonna tell me?"

"I'm tellin' you now, Arlis." Longarm gave her a commanding look. "Tomorrow, we fork trails. You go on back to the Cross Fire. Oughta be safe enough—you made it all the way to Denver by yourself, after all."

Arlis hardened her jaw and shook her head. "Uh-uh. No way. I'm going up trail with you, Longarm. Del Sager killed my pa, and if I can't kill him myself, I sure as shit up a cow's ass am gonna be there when he gets it, so I can watch the scoundrel die and laugh just before he shakes hands with the Devil."

That was just the point of view Longarm had been afraid of. Likely, she'd have wanted to follow him out of Lightning Flat, as well.

He walked over to her, put his hands on her shoulders, and planted a kiss on her forehead. "I can understand that, Arlis. Truly I can. But you gotta let me do my work, and I won't be able to do it if I gotta worry about your safety."

Arlis stepped back and crossed her arms on her breasts, staring up at him stubbornly. "You don't have to worry about my safety. I can fend for myself."

"Like you fended for yourself this afternoon, downstairs?"

"Them tinhorns caught me by surprise."

Longarm shook his head. "You sleep in tomorrow, have a good breakfast, then head on back to Lightning Flat and your ranch. When I've run Sager to ground, I'll ride over and tell you in person."

She continued to give him a cold glare. Gradually, however, her eyes lost their hardness, and she turned her mouth corners down as she swung away and pounded her door in defeat. "Ah, hell! I suppose you're right. I reckon I would just slow you down, wouldn't I?"

"I reckon you could."

"I reckon you'd best keep your full attention on Sager, and not have to worry about me. Ah, shit. Well, damnit, Longarm—how're you so sure you're gonna be able to run them owlhoots to ground all by your lonesome, anyway? I mean, you're mighty good with that six-shooter—I seen that—but Sager's got a good seven, eight men ridin' for him. And then you're gonna have to manage his brother, too, you say?"

Longarm gave the girl a cockeyed smile, nudged her chin up with his thumb, and left her with one last parting kiss on her warm, welcoming mouth. "You let me worry about that. I'll manage. I have before. Sometimes one man's better'n a whole army."

He turned away from her and started back to his own door.

"Hey, Longarm?"

He turned back to her. She grinned and arched a brow at him cunningly. "Want another tussle for the road? Might make it easier for you to concentrate on Sager later."

"Good lord, girl." Longarm chuffed in mock reproof as he pushed his door open. "I don't know who's more dangerous—you or Sager!"

Longarm tramped into his room, closed his door and locked it, and had a nightcap before collapsing in his bed, half-clothed and falling instantly into a long, dreamless sleep. He was awake at first cockcrow—and there indeed was a cock crowing in a coop somewhere behind the hotel.

When Longarm looked out, he saw that it was still mostly night, with only a faint lilac flush in the west and an even fainter pink blush in the east behind a line of hills known as the Salamander Buttes. He could hear the German woman back there, stomping around while she fed her hogs and chickens. Longarm got up, pulled the rest of his clothes on, rinsed his mouth with the cheap whiskey he'd bought from Lawton, spit it into a thunder mug, and then imbibed a deep pull. The forty-rod seemed to clear the cobwebs from the night's deep sleep and open his lungs, making him just a tad more awake and alert than he would have been otherwise—or so he told himself.

He stuffed the bottle into his war bag, from which he produced a few bits of jerky and hardtack left over from his New Mexico assignment, and donned his hat. Nibbling the breakfast, he shouldered his gear and stepped quietly into the hall, glad to see Arlis's door closed and to not hear any sounds of her early rising behind it. He headed on downstairs, crossed the dark saloon hall where all the chairs were overturned onto tables for sleeping, and there were no signs of Lawton or anyone else.

Munching jerky, Longarm tramped over to the livery barn and found the bulldog-tough little kid up and already hard at work. Longarm saddled the mount while the boy—Buster was his name—told him about the only trail heading north out of Hope Springs, and that the trail forked off to several ranches but also snaked forever northward into the Bear Lodge Mountains. Longarm had figured there wouldn't be more than one, and he was glad to know which trail that Little Louis had likely taken on his way to meet his brother.

Longarm bid the boy adieu as he mounted the gray; then he pressed his heels to the horse's flanks and loped westward along the north edge of the sleeping little backwater town, only a few breakfast fires pushing smoke up from chimney pipes and touching the cool, fresh air with the smell of ham and bacon. He found the trail in the scrub between the town and the cavalry post, and snorted when he saw the post's lone sentry tipped back in a chair against the side of the officer's quarters—or deceased officer's quarters, as it was—sound asleep beneath his down-tipped hat brim, an old Springfield rifle resting across his thighs, an uncorked bottle at his feet. Longarm tore another piece of jerky off the strip he was work-

ing on and put the gray into a hard lope along the trail
that stretched off over the sage-stippled hills that were
gradually lightening as the sun poked its molten yellow
head above the horizon.

Two long, hot, dusty days later, Longarm spied vultures
circling above a wash just ahead of his position and to
the right of the powdery horse trail he'd been following.
He rode into the scrub brush and rocks, passing a lone
cottonwood filled with quarreling blackbirds, and drew
rein on the lip of the wash.

Six or seven turkey buzzards squawked indignantly,
jerking their bald heads and beady, copper eyes toward
the interloper. They took awkward flight, heavy wings
beating the dry air and kicking up dust in little cyclones.
They stirred up the sweet smell of death, and Longarm
lifted his green silk neckerchief to cover his nose against
the stench. His right hand automatically slid across his
belly to close around the walnut grips of his double-
action .44 when he saw the three dead men lying at the
bottom of the wash.

Two Mexicans and one white man with sun-bleached
blond hair.

They lay side-by-side, heads propped up against the
gravelly opposite side of the cut, gloved hands in their
laps. They could have been resting there, but the bullet
holes that had been widened by the probing, hungry
beaks of the buzzards gave the lie to that impression.

Three of the six eyes had been plucked from their
sockets. One hung down a sun-blackened cheek by a
grisly red thread.

Longarm lifted his eyes from the wash and looked

around cautiously. He spied no movement but the slight ruffling of the yucca and greasewood branches and the buzzards gathering to berate the intruder from perches high in the barren branches of a dead sycamore. He hadn't expected to see anyone lingering around the stench emanating from the gravelly wash. Only carrion-eaters could stomach such a smell.

Whoever had killed the three dead men—all of whom were dressed in worn trail clothes but with well-kept holsters on their hips and oiled shell belts around their waists—were long gone. They'd taken the men's bullets and guns. In one case, they'd even taken a pair of boots, leaving one of the Mexicans in his red stocking feet, his big right toe poking up from a sizeable hole. The dead men's hats were gone, but they might have blown off when the men had so violently given up their ghosts.

They might have been rustlers, but Longarm hadn't seen any cattle since last night. Likely, these three were long-coulee riders who'd crossed trails with more of their ilk and swapped some lead. It happened all the time, badmen challenging badmen for no other reason than they were all bad men and liked nothing more than a challenge.

Had the killers been from Little Louis's band?

Longarm's blood quickened slightly. He hadn't run into any tracks along the trail he'd been following, only a few dried horse apples and the remains of a cook fire. He'd hoped like hell he'd been on the right trail, and seeing the three dead men here was encouraging. Whoever had killed them had been good, better than these gunmen themselves had been.

Longarm reined the gray back to the main trail and

continued angling north by northeast, rising and falling over the barren, rocky buttes that seemed to roll on forever across the greasewood-stippled wastes. Only a couple of hours later, he came upon the faint tracks of several riders. Farther on, the tracks grew plainer, more recent. He also discovered the remains of a cook fire in another shallow wash, as well as charred antelope bones and a peach tin.

Continuing on up the trail, he counted eight sets of hoofprints.

Gradually, he was catching up to whoever was on the trail ahead of him. He hoped like hell it was Little Louis.

He took time to snare a couple of jackrabbits, then camped that night in a hollow at the base of a sandstone butte, lulled to sleep by the distant howling of prowling wolves. He was on the trail the next morning before the sun had yet swallowed the bulky purple shadows angling out from the spare trees, boulders, and craggy-topped bluffs.

Around ten o'clock that morning he rode into the sun-parched yard of a stage relay station. The tracks he'd been following, including half a dozen piles of fresh horse apples that had lent their own perfume to the tang of sage and greasewood, led up to the weathered brick, sod-roofed station house on the left side of the yard, under a steep sandstone ridge.

There, eight sweat-lathered horses stood tied beneath an arbor of slim, woven aspen branches, swishing their tails at flies.

Chapter 10

Longarm rode on up to the hitchrack and put the gray into the shade beneath the arbor. The other horses turned to glance at the newcomer and a few switched their tales more vigorously in greeting. One gave a whinny. The gray answered in kind. Longarm didn't mind. If he was trailing the man he hoped he was, his presence in the yard was already known.

Likely, the men inside the station house had spied him trailing them by now, as well. He kept his deputy U.S. marshal's badge in his coat pocket, and, casting a glance at the dusty, sashed window to the left of the timbered front door and seeing nothing but dust and the silver against black of reflected sunlight, he slid his Winchester from its saddle scabbard. He didn't rack a shell into the chamber, though he badly wanted to. If it was going to be eight against one, he needed all the help he could get. But racking the shell would likely have been noted, and have marked him as certain trouble.

Instead, he casually set the rifle atop his shoulder, fished in the breast pocket of his sweat-damp shirt for a three-for-a-nickel cheroot, bit the end off, and stuck it into his mouth. He stepped between the two hitchracks and mounted the low gallery, pulling a stove match out of his pants pocket. Pulling the timbered door open and grinding his teeth at the grate of its unoiled hinges, while hoping like hell he wasn't met with a barrage of lead bumblebees from inside, he stepped as casually as he could over the threshold and pulled the door closed behind him.

"That's all right, mister," said a voice from somewhere ahead of him and to the left. "You can leave it open. We need a little air in here."

Longarm took a cursory look around, saw several rugged faces staring at him blandly, as well as the prissier, paler face of the bowler-hatted gent behind the bar, and stepped back outside to kick a broken brick into place to hold the door open. When he was sure the door would stay, he went back inside, stepped to the left of the door and out of the breeze, and scratched his match to light on his thumbnail.

Cupping the match to the end of his cigar, he feigned an offhand air as he glanced around the room through the gray smoke puffs and counted five men in addition to the barman—four playing cards at a large round table in the room's middle and one more standing at the bar, leaning forward, elbows resting atop the polished mahogany that looked as out of place as Cynthia Larimer would have looked out here. As he waved the match out and turned to flick it back into the dust beyond the gallery, Longarm reflected that he'd been wrong. No one appeared to have been keeping watch, unless the sixth, seventh, and eighth riders were scouting the yard from somewhere he couldn't see.

Disappointment was a chord jerking taut in his belly. You'd think Little Louis would be more careful than that. Maybe Longarm hadn't been trailing Little Louis, after all. Certainly none of the faces around him resembled the gopherish countenance he remembered from wanted circulars. Maybe he'd come this far through the dusty heart of the eastern Wyoming desert on a wild goose chase.

No one said anything as Longarm, maintaining a casual air, tramped slowly toward the bar while puffing his cheroot. He wished he knew where the other three riders were. Behind the fancy bar, an even fancier, gold-framed oval clock ticked on the pine-paneled wall. The barman stood in front of the lone man on Longarm's side of the bar, regarding Longarm expectantly, a stove match clamped down hard in one corner of his mouth. He was wearing a deerskin vest and a low apron, a stained towel dangling from behind it. The customer standing at the bar glanced at Longarm over his shoulder, then quickly returned his gaze to the top of the spotless mahogany.

The card players each twisted or lifted a glance at him and then continued playing. Finally, the barman cleared his throat, stretched a waxy smile on his clean-shaven face, and stepped down the bar toward Longarm. "Hot out there."

"Hot an' dusty," Longarm said, setting his rifle onto the bar while noting that the man standing to his right had done the same with his own Henry repeater. "I could use some of that dust cut with a shot of good rye."

He rolled his eyes farther right and saw that the card players all had rifles within easy reach, as well. Some of the long guns leaned against the table or lay across otherwise empty chairs. Apprehension was a single, cold raindrop dribbling down the back of Longarm's neck.

"Sure, sure," said the barman, glancing at the other customer at the bar and reaching beneath the bar for a bottle.

He smiled affably as he pulled a shot glass down from a pyramid stacked between Longarm and the other standing hombre, uncorked the bottle, and splashed some cheap rye into the glass. Expertly, he slid the glass across the bar to Longarm without spilling a drop, then set the bottle down in front of him. He didn't put the cork back in the bottle. Instead, he just stood there between Longarm and the other man, smiling woodenly down at the bottle as though waiting for it to say something.

His Adam's apple rose and fell heavily as he swallowed.

His left hand, which held the cork on top of the bar, shook ever so faintly.

"Cheers." Longarm threw back the shot.

He caught a flash of light in the pale face of the clock behind the bar, and before he'd set the glass down on the bar top, he raked his right hand across his belly and filled it with the cool, worn, familiar grips of his Colt .44. He jerked the piece out of its holster and whipped it off to his right, where he saw the other bar customer making much the same movement while bringing a silver-chased Russian .44 to bear on Longarm.

Longarm's revolver exploded first. A quarter second

later, the Russian thundered. The window behind Longarm shattered. At the same time the man with the Russian jerked his head up and crossed his eyes as if to see
the quarter-sized hole in his forehead, while his battered
Stetson fell forward off his head, bounced off his chest,
and landed on the floor at his feet.

Longarm didn't see the hat land. Sensing sudden
movement behind him and hearing the raucous scrape of
several chairs across the floor and the thump of boots as
men bolted to their feet, he grabbed his Winchester,
leaped straight up off his heels, and dove over the bar.
He cleared the top of it just as a cannonade of rifles and
pistols filled the room with an ear-rending thunder.

He hit the floor on the other side as glass and whiskey rained down from the shelves above him—not rained
so much as stormed, pelting his now-hatless head, soak-
ing his hair and shoulders. As the lead continued to hammer the bar, and the wall and shelves and clock behind
it, Longarm heaved himself up off an elbow. His boots
ground the broken glass that now virtually covered the
floor. Glancing to his right, he saw the barman lying back
against the front wall, right of the window, one bullet
through his forehead, another through his right eye, all
limbs hanging limp.

Biting back a curse at the savagery at the killers' fu-
sillade, Longarm pushed up to a crouch, careful to keep
his head just below the level of the bar, from which
wood slivers and shards from the glass pyramid still flew
in all directions to bounce off the wall behind him. He
waited for a slight lull in the shooting, then jerked his
head and arm up and fired two shots quickly, missing his
targets but at least getting an idea of where the four

shooters were—spread out around the table they'd been sitting at, two wielding rifles, the two others pistols.

One shouted and jerked his pistol toward Longarm just as the lawman tucked his head back down behind the bar. He scuttled forward at a low crouch as bullets pelted the wall before which he'd just been standing.

Six feet beyond his previous position, he rose again, fired three more quick shots, then, hearing an indignant yelp from among his would-be executioners, dropped to a knee and holstered the empty Colt. He felt the burn of a graze across his left cheek, dribbling blood down his jawline.

Grabbing his Winchester, he swung around and crabbed back in the other direction behind the bar, toward the front wall. There was a three-foot gap between the bar and the wall, near where the dead barman lay, lower jaw hanging, head canted onto his right shoulder. Longarm stopped there, waiting, noting another gradual slowing in the savage fire.

"You had better days, amigo?" he asked the dead barman, racking a round into the Winchester's chamber. "Yeah, me too."

The gunfire died. He heard a couple of hammers click on empty chambers. He also heard one of the men whisper. A floorboard creaked. There was the snick of a gun being slid into a holster.

Longarm bolted up from behind the end of the bar and quickly took in the positions of the four men—one reaching tensely for a pistol on the table they'd been playing cards at, another moving toward the bar on the balls of his boots and lifting his head to peer behind it. Longarm shot the man going for the gun on the table first, the man nearest the bar second, before either had time to turn toward him.

The other two swung around, yelling anxiously, one racking a fresh round into his Winchester carbine. Only one got a shot off, this one clinking through a glass shard remaining in the window behind Longarm and spanging off a porch post beyond it, before Longarm drilled the man through the center of his chest. Dust puffed from his calico shirt as he flew backward, screaming and throwing his rifle in the air.

Longarm's fourth shot plunked through the throat of the fourth and final gent, who then blew a hole through his own foot with one of the two long-barreled revolvers in his hands. He was a Mexican in a steeple-crowned sombrero, and his hat tumbled down his back as he jumped high on his feet and wheeled, hopping around while clutching his blood-spewing throat with both hands, shouting raspy Spanish epithets.

Longarm strode forward, stopped once more, racked a fresh shell into the Winchester's breech, then drilled the Mex through his left ear. The bullet exited his right ear and chewed a dogget of slivers from a ceiling support post. It also shut the man up and sat him down in a chair, where he sat for a full five seconds before tumbling slowly forward and rolling down to the floor, where he promptly farted, jerked, and died.

Longarm lowered the smoking Winchester from his shoulder. Striding slowly forward, he thumbed fresh shells through the rifle's loading gate. He kicked over a couple of the dead men, giving each a close inspection. None appeared anything like Little Louis.

So where was the gopher-faced little killer, anyway?

And the other two riders?

As if in response to his question, door hinges squawked softly behind a deerskin curtain at the back of the room. A man's thin, trembling, slightly girlish voice said, "Ralph? Connors?"

Longarm stepped sideways, out of line of fire from the room or the hall behind the curtain, and pressed a shoulder against the brick wall to the right of it.

"Hey, Tomas!" the voice called, louder, more impatient.

Frightened.

Longarm said in voice pitched low with steely calm, "Your friends done gone to see Jesus, Little Louis. Come on out here. Let's palaver."

A pistol popped three times, drilling three holes through the deerskin curtain, making it ruffle. The slugs tore across the main room and thumped into the front wall.

Longarm jerked his head around the door casing, shoving the curtain aside with his head and peering down a dingy hall. A man stood about ten feet away, outside an open door on the hall's right side. He looked like he'd just gotten up. A window from inside the room showed mussed hair and jeans pulled on over balbriggans. He was barefoot, and he stood about five-nine or five-ten. His face was partially silhouetted, but it was round, with thick lips and prominent front teeth. A little pot gut pushed against his threadbare undershirt.

Just as Longarm began to bring his Winchester up, Little Louis leaped back into the room behind him and out of sight. A girl groaned. She was shoved into the hall, and Little Louis followed. He held her tightly around the waist, pressing her nearly naked body against his, shieldlike, while holding a cocked pistol to her right temple. A black-haired, black-eyed girl, she wore only a gauzy night wrap, one strap hanging from a shoulder. Her skin was dusky behind the see-through wrap, the pale light from the room silhouetting deep, pendulous breasts.

Little Louis gritted his teeth. "Throw that rifle down, or I'm gonna blow this poor girl's brains out!"

Longarm thought it over for about two seconds. He grinned and aimed his Winchester straight down the hall, narrowing his right eye as he planted the rifle's sites on Louis's forehead. "Drill her."

The girl's black eyes snapped wide.

Louis frowned. "Huh? You hear me, mister? I'm gonna kill this little bitch if'n you don't put that Winny down right now!"

"Go ahead."

Longarm stared down the dim hall at Little Louis and the girl. The girl stared back in horror. Gradually, the horror turned to frustration, and then she reached up and slid Little Louis's cocked pistol away from her head. "Forget it, stupid shit. He knows the score."

Little Louis's gopherish face acquired an exasperated look, forked veins in his forehead swelling. "Who the fuck are you? Law?"

"That's right. Here to take you in, Louis. You got warrants on you as long as the look on your *puta*'s face."

Louis sighed and lowered the pistol to his side, depressing the hammer with a ratcheting click. "How'd you know?"

"Eight horses outside. Five dead men behind me. Two

of you makes seven. Besides, I was told you're traveling with a Mexican whore."

"I am not a whore!" spat the *puta*, leaning forward at the waist, her black eyes glinting like small-caliber pistols. "I am his sweetheart. We are going to be married— Louis an' me."

"That's right touching. I can just hear them wedding bells now."

Longarm moved down the hall toward the two, keeping an eye on the open door of the room to the right. He shoved Louis around by a shoulder. "Belly down on the floor, asshole. You too, *puta*."

"I told you . . . !"

Longarm grabbed the back of her neck and shoved her down to her bare knees. "Down!"

As he drove her down on her belly, she screamed and called him several nasty names in Spanish.

He grabbed one set of handcuffs from the back of his cartridge belt and closed them around Little Louis's narrow, almost delicate wrists. "Where's the eighth man in your group?" he grunted, looking around cautiously, half-expecting a rifle to be aimed through the doorway behind him.

"Eighth?" Louis glanced at the girl on the floor beside him in mock befuddlement. "Were we ridin' with eight, Esmeralda?"

"Eight?" The girl frowned, falling right in with Louis's little joke. "No, no," she drawled in heavily accented English. "You got that wrong, big lawman, sir. You can't count, I think."

Longarm had another set of handcuffs in his saddlebags. To secure the girl for now, he ripped off his neckerchief and used it to tie her wrists together. Rising and turning toward the open room, he said, "You two stay there. Keep your heads down. One move out of either one of you, I'll drill you. I make no exceptions for women."

"That does not surprise me!" spat the whore, lifting her chin from the floor and gritting her teeth at Longarm.

Chapter 11

When Longarm had checked the room in which Little Louis Estevez and his buxom pal Esmeralda had been holed up during the shooting, and found nothing there but one dead rat in a trap and the lingering smell of cheap whiskey and sex, he hazed both owlhoots into the main part of the station house at the point of his Winchester.

"Do you think I could dress?" Esmeralda growled. "I'm all but naked, for the love of Jesus!"

"Noticed that."

"Holy shit," Louis whistled, looking around the main room in awe. "You done killed 'em all, didn't ya?"

"All except for you two and the eighth man. Now, you gonna tell me—?"

Something smacked into a ceiling joist a few feet in front of Longarm, between him and his two prisoners. Dust wafted down as the post shuddered audibly. Both Louis and Esmeralda ducked with starts, the puta curs-

ing loudly, as the rifle report echoed from somewhere
out in the yard.

Longarm stepped back, glancing out the window left
of the door while keeping his Winchester aimed at his
prisoners.

"Goddamnit, Jeston!" Louis bawled, sort of crouching and staring out the same window as Longarm, his
hands cuffed behind his back. "Hold your goddamn fire!
You damn near drilled me and Esmeralda!"

As Longarm stared out the dusty window, he saw a
vague figure standing in the shade off the northeast corner of the barn. A horse flanked him, looking jittery.

"That you, Louis?" the man shouted.

"Yeah, it's me. Me an' Esmeralda's the only ones
alive in here. 'Ceptin' for the tall, badge-totin' drink of
water holdin' a Winny on us. I'm guessin' federal—he's
got that look about him!" Louis chuckled and gave Longarm a mocking look over his shoulder.

"You want me to come in there?" called the man outside, sounding tough.

"Nah, I don't think so, Jes. This one here's a little
more serious than most o' the other lawdogs we run into
of late." Again, Louis gave Longarm a dubious look over
his shoulder. Then he turned back toward the window.
"That your horse out there?" he yelled.

"Yeah, I got ole Frisco with me."

"Mount up an' fetch Del. Powder the trail, Jes. Del'll
know what to do."

This time both Louis and Esmeralda cast Longarm
devious glances over their shoulders. Longarm tried not
to look pleased, but that's just how he felt. He'd thought

he would have to beat Louis with his pistol, till he had only a few ribbons of flesh left hanging from his ugly, buck-toothed mug, before he'd get the little killer to lead Longarm to his brother's hideout. But now Louis was going to bring Del Sager to him, and all Longarm likely had to do was wait.

Louis laughed and turned to the window. "I think he recognized my brother's name, Jes. Think he mighta just dribbled down his leg. Ha! Ride on outta here, Jes! Fetch my brother—Del Sager! Bring him and his whole damn gang!"

Outside, the man by the barn turned away from the station house and swung up onto his dun. "I'll do that, Louis. We'll track ya from here. Don't you worry none. Like you said, Del'll know what to do!"

With that he ground spurs into his dun's flanks, and the horse bounded off its rear hooves and away from the station house. Tan dust sifted behind him. Gradually, the thud of galloping hooves dwindled, and there was only the sound of the flies buzzing around the spilled blood in the station house.

"Well, at least the eighth man is accounted for," Longarm said.

"I'll say he is," Louis chuckled. "Ole Jeston was in the barn, havin' him a nap. Little too much of the who-hit-john last night, don't ya know. Figure he shoulda helped out in the fight. Cowardly streak, I reckon. I'll kill him later."

Louis grinned. It faded when Longarm said, "At least he wasn't holed up back there with a whore, Louis."

"You just wait, lawdog," Louis snarled, narrowing an

eye and bulging that forked vein in his forehead again.
"You're gonna be goddamn sorry you tussled with the
Sager boys."

Longarm sighed. "Yeah, well—we all step in it now
an' then."

Esmeralda pressed her lips together, giving Longarm
a menacing look of dark foreboding. She wasn't a bad-
looking girl. Even features and long, black hair. But she
would have been better off without the small pockmarks
on the nubs of her cheeks, and she was missing an eye-
tooth. Amazing how a single missing tooth could uglify
a woman. Nice tits, though. Longarm reckoned they were
why she was here, riding with Little Louis Estevez.

"Might as well get dressed now, Esmeralda." Longarm stepped to one side and gestured with his rifle at
the deerskin curtain over the doorway behind them. "You
don't mind if Louis and I watch, do you? Nothing per-
sonal, you understand."

Esmeralda spat viciously and stomped past him, heavy
breasts swinging behind her wrap. Louis laughed and
shook his head as he stared after her, smitten.

When Longarm had gotten both his prisoners fully dressed
and ready to ride, he chained them back-to-back to a
ceiling joist in the main room of the station house. Then
he dragged the dead station manager, who apparently
ran the place alone, outside and buried him behind the
cabin, fashioning a marker with two cottonwood branches
and rope. The poor man had merely been in the wrong
place at the wrong time, and he deserved the best burial
Longarm could give him.

As for the dead outlaws, they deserved to rot where

they lay, but Longarm grudgingly dragged them all outside and rolled them into a ravine on the east side of the yard, thus saving whoever came next to tend the station from being greeted by five smelly corpses.

As he worked, he thought over a course of action. He decided to trail Little Louis and Esmeralda to Belle Fourche on the Wyoming-Dakota border, about a hundred miles east, and turn them over to the law there for safekeeping. He was on good terms with the sheriff, Ed Hinkle, an old border bandit himself, as was Hinkle's deputy, Craw Cirrus. The two men's outlaw days were long over, and over the past several years they'd both proven to be good, dependable lawmen. They'd held down the proverbial fort of Belle Fourche, in the heart of outlaw and Indian country, for more years than most lawmen stayed alive in that neck of the woods.

Longarm couldn't think of two more capable lawbringers to back his play against Del Sager. He hoped to lead Sager right into Belle Fourche—or close to it, anyway—where, with the help of the Belle Fourche lawdogs, Longarm would bring him and his gang down once and for all. Of course, that might prove to be a lot easier intended than done . . .

First, he had to consider the stage station, which would now be unattended for a while. According to a timetable he'd found in the lodge, another stage wasn't due for four days. Longarm would pass the word of the attendant's death to the next manager along the line, as he planned to take the stage road to Belle Fourche and thus give Sager an easy trail to follow. He figured the fresh team of stage horses in the holding corral would be all right until someone came to replace the dead man. To make sure they were, he forked hay into their feeding crib, filled their trough with water from a rain barrel, and filled several feeding buckets with extra water, as well.

Then he unsaddled and released all the outlaw horses except Little Louis's black and Esmeralda's brown-and-white pinto, confiscating the knives and pistols he found in their saddlebags, and released his two charges from their ceiling joist. He hazed them outside, into the bright sunlight, and removed their cuffs long enough for each to mount up and get comfortable.

He was sweating from the couple of hours' work, his shirt pasted against his back.

"Hey, lawdog," Esmeralda said, shaking her hair back from her face and giving him a flirty look. She wore a green felt Stetson with a braided leather band and a red-and-black calico blouse which she'd left open halfway down her deep, dark cleavage. "You got a name?"

"We gonna be friends now, Esmeralda?" Longarm tossed a pair of cuffs to her, aiming his rifle at her casually from his hip while puffing a cheroot clamped between his teeth.

"Sure, why not?" she said, twirling the cuffs on one finger. "These are not really necessary, are they?"

He rolled the cheroot from one side of his mouth to the other. "Oh, I disagree, *chiquita*."

"What do you say you and I talk about this, no? Privately. We could go back into the station house and maybe have a drink together, uh? Louis wouldn't mind . . . if we struck a deal . . ."

Longarm glanced at Louis, who grinned from his saddle. The gopher-faced outlaw was leaning forward, his cuffed hands wrapped around the horn.

Turning back to Esmeralda, Longarm said, "You must be one helluva piece of ass."

Her eyes glinted alluringly, and she threw her shoulders back, breasts forward. "Oh, I am."

"She ain't lyin', lawdog," Louis said. "She'll fuck you . . . if you promise to turn us loose. It'll be worth it. You'll see. I mean, it ain't really much of a decision, when you think real hard on it. My brother ain't holed up far from here. I figure you're gonna be one howlin', dyin' lawdog before noon tomorrow at the latest. Look at it this way—you'll be getting' a piece of the best Mexican tail in all of Sonora, and your life in the bargain."

Louis winked.

Esmeralda dropped her chin and favored Longarm with a smoldering look, letting her eyes flicker tauntingly across his crotch.

"I thought you two was gettin' married," Longarm said.

"What's that got to with anything?" Louis said.

"I sure would hate to be a home wrecker." Longarm narrowed an eye and thumbed back the Winchester's barrel as he aimed the rifle at Esmeralda's cleavage. "Now, you put that bracelet on, Esmeralda, or I'll drill a hole between those pretty tits of yours." He grinned when, scowling at him furiously, she clicked the cuffs closed around her wrists. "And you can call me Longarm, seein' as how we're gonna be partnered up for a few days."

She spat angrily in the dust at his feet.

Louis laughed without mirth and scrunched up his sunburned wedge of a nose. "Bad decision, Longarm. Bad, bad decision."

"It's hot and I'm tired, and here it's only a little past noon." Longarm mounted the gray and took the reins of his prisoners' horses in his left hand. He gave Louis a hard look. "So don't fuck with me. I'm liable to shoot you both for resisting arrest, and dump you in a ravine."

Louis and Esmeralda scowled at him but said nothing. Reining the gray eastward, he nudged his heels against the horse's flanks and led off at a trot, tugging his prisoners' horses along behind him. As he rode by some creek he didn't know the name of, twisting along low, sun-baked buttes spiked with sparse patches of yucca, he couldn't help casting furtive, wary glances behind him now and then. He had no idea how far from the stage station Sager was holed up. Louis had said he wasn't far, but Longarm couldn't rely on anything Louis said. For all he knew, Sager's current hideout lay in the heart of the Bear Lodge Mountains, a good two, three days' ride away.

On the other hand, he might be only a couple of hours away.

If so, Sager might just show up on Longarm's back trail any old time. When he did, Longarm needed to be ready. He'd been told Sager rode with eight men. Those weren't much longer odds than Longarm had faced in the station house back yonder. But out here in the open might be a different story entirely . . .

And he had Little Louis and Esmeralda to contend with.

He rubbed his cheroot out against his saddle skirt and stuffed it into his shirt pocket, hoping he got his two charges to Belle Fourche before Sager showed.

The stage road rose and fell across a rugged patch of

chalky badlands. It was a hard ride, the sun beating down mercilessly, the smell of hot sage peppering Longarm's nose. He looked directly behind from time to time. Both Little Louis and Esmeralda rode sleeping in their saddles, heads flopping. Must have had a hard night and an even harder morning. Beyond them, the trail spooled back toward the station house and the carnage Longarm had left there.

Nothing within the lawman's sight but the sun-scorched hills punctuated by empty sage flats, the only movement being a few hunting hawks and jackrabbits nibbling bunchgrass.

About halfway between relay stations, he figured, they came upon a water hole. It was fed by a spring dribbling down from rocks in the side of a bluff. Longarm reined the horses to a halt, tied them to a gnarled cedar, and held his rifle on Little Louis and Esmeralda.

"Climb down. Any sudden moves, and—"

"I know, I know," Esmeralda drawled, looking tired and drawn. "You'll drill a hole between my pretty *chiconas.*" She stretched her lips slightly. Her eyes flashed at him. She and Louis swung down from their saddles.

"One at a time," Longarm said, gesturing at the muddy brown water with his Winchester. He curled his upper lip. "Ladies first, I reckon."

"Ain't no ladies here," Louis said, favoring the girl with his gopherish, mocking grin.

Esmeralda didn't take kindly to the jibe. "Shut up, asshole. You are why we are out here, Louis!"

Little Louis dropped his jaw, indignant. "Hey, don't get sore at me, honey!"

"Fuck you, Louis!" Esmeralda's fiery temper ex-

ploded, and she leaned toward the fat-faced outlaw, who
was an inch or so shorter than she was, and shouted several Spanish epithets before "You should have gone into
the main room and helped the others. I doubt it would
have made any difference." She jerked her head at Longarm. "He's obviously three times the man you are, but
who knows, you might have got lucky!"

Louis just stared at her, those forking veins in his
forehead bulging.

"Hey, Longarm," Esmeralda said, lifting one mouth
corner. "You know why they call him Little Louis?"

Longarm groaned. "Ah shit."

Chapter 12

"You fuckin' bitch!" Little Louis railed at his Mexican wife-to-be.

But before he could raise his cuffed hands to smack her across the face, Longarm grabbed the outlaw by the back of his shirt collar and flung him to the ground. Dust rose. Little Louis squealed and coughed.

Esmeralda laughed.

"I think I liked you two better when you were against me together."

Louis called Longarm several names. The lawman ignored him and ordered Esmeralda to get her drink at the water hole. As she turned away, glaring at Louis, who lay in the dirt where Longarm had deposited him and glared back at her, the lawman went over and loosened the saddle cinches on his and the other two mounts, giving the horses a breather.

He'd grabbed his canteen from his saddle and was

heading over toward a flat rock sitting in the shade beneath a spindly cottonwood, when Esmeralda called behind him, "Hey, Longarm."

"What?" Tired of these two already, he turned to look over at her. His throat tightened. She'd opened her shirt and drawn the straps of her lace-edged, pink camisole down her arms, exposing all but the very tips of her breasts. She was on her knees beside the water hole, holding her cuffed hands out.

"Why don't you come over here and take these cuffs off. I'd like to bathe properly." Esmeralda sneered at Louis. "Like a lady."

"Forget it." Longarm sat down on the rock and popped the cork from his canteen.

"Come on, lawman," Esmeralda urged, turning so that she was almost facing him, the camisole clinging to her nipples. She pushed her shoulders forward and lifted her hands in supplication and pleading, squeezing her large orbs together invitingly. "What can it hurt to turn me loose? I am unarmed. I won't try to run from you. You are the only man out here. I could fall prey to the savages that haunt this part of the country."

"Esmeralda," Little Louis growled, narrowing an eye at the girl kneeling half-naked by the waterhole. "If we ever get out of this, I'm gonna braid those purty tits of yours. Can't you see he ain't interested?"

"I just want my hands free so that I can splash water on my chest." She was staring at Longarm, stretching her lips and apparently not self-conscious about showing the gap of her missing upper tooth. "Unless you'd like to come over and do it for me. No tricks, lawdog. Shit, I don't care what happens to Louis. Me—I haven't done anything to go to jail for. Lock him up for as long as you want."

"I'm gonna give you one more minute over there," Longarm said, impatient. "Then it's Louis's turn. Then we're hitting the trail."

He lifted the canteen and took a pull of the tepid water. As he did, he caught a glimpse of dust rising to his right, along their back trail that snaked off between the chalky buttes. He lowered the canteen and stared at the sifting dust until it had settled.

Apprehension pulled at him. Narrowing each eye in turn, he looked around. Could have been only a dust devil.

But he couldn't ignore the needling suspicion scratching at his spine.

Casually, he rose from the rock and walked over to his horse. "Esmeralda," he said, "get your ass back over to Louis."

"Fuck Louis!"

Longarm grabbed the rope off his saddle horn.

"I didn't say fuck Louis—I said get over and sit down beside him. Shut up and be quick about it, or I'll drill a bullet through one of those tits you're so damn proud of."

She had no hurry in her, so he walked over and grabbed her and half-dragged her to where Louis sat now on his butt, knees up, looking at Longarm with a befuddled cast to his otherwise cow-stupid gaze. Quickly, Longarm tied them back-to-back, the girl groaning and grunting indignantly, Louis saying, "What's the matter, lawman? You see a ghost back there, did you?"

"Both of you keep quiet. One word out of either one

of you, I'll drill you through an eyeball. No hesitation whatsoever. Understand?"

They both glowered at him. Longarm grabbed his rifle and, glancing along their backtrail once more, slipped into a northern crease between the buttes. He quietly racked a fresh round into the Winchester's breech as he followed the narrow crease to another one that intersected the first and was spotted with old cow manure and fresher deer pellets.

He took the intersecting crease westward for about forty yards, then turned back toward the canyon containing the water hole. Coming around the shoulder of an eroded bluff, he stopped suddenly. A figure stood before him, in the shade of a large cottonwood whose silver leaves fluttered in a dry breeze. The person's slender back faced him as he stared toward the water hole from behind the tree, long brown hair blowing in the breeze.

Stepping slowly forward, Longarm snugged his Winchester's barrel up against the back of the shadower's neck. He snarled through gritted teeth, "Hold it right there, you little sidewinder."

The shadower jerked with a start and swung around, hazel eyes wide with shock. But then they softened, and a warm smile spread her lips.

"Hidy!"

Longarm depressed the Winchester's hammer. "Goddamnit, Arlis. What in the holy hell are you doin' out here?"

"Followin' you, of course," she said brashly.

"I can see that. Why? I thought we had an agreement. You were supposed to leave Hope Springs and head your little fanny straight back to the Cross Fire."

The girl cocked a leg and folded her hands defiantly on her chest. "Never intended to. I figured on followin' you straight into the den of that devil, Del Sager, all along. Knew you wouldn't let me, so I followed you a couple hours back. Did a pretty good job, too, even if I do say so myself. You had no idea I was back there, didja?"

"That ain't the goddamn point, you pesky little brat."

"You didn't think I was so pesky the other night," she said smugly.

"That mistake is long since over." Longarm laid the rifle on his shoulder. "You get back on your horse and head the hell out of here."

Ignoring the order, she said, "I seen the blood in the station back yonder. You clean up right well, don't you?" She canted her head toward Longarm's prisoners. "Is that buck-toothed urchin with the sandy hair Little Louis?"

"None of your goddamn business!" Exasperated, wondering how in hell he was going to get rid of the girl, Longarm brushed past her and headed back toward the water hole.

He heard her stride along behind him, heels grinding gravel. "The woman part of his gang?"

Longarm said nothing. He strode past Little Louis and Esmeralda, both of whom studied Arlis Pine with interest. "Lookee there," the gopher-faced outlaw said. "Another girl. That's good, 'cause I'm done with this one here."

Esmeralda jerked around to give him a jab with both her elbows.

"Ow!" Louis squawked.

Arlis stood a few feet from the pair, looking down at

them like she'd just found a dead rattlesnake. "Damn, he don't look no bigger than me."

Longarm slid his rifle back into his saddle boot, then whipped around and grabbed the girl's elbow. He led her back the way they'd come, grinding his molars. "Arlis, if you don't head back to the Cross Fire right now . . ." He hesitated, feeling his ears burn.

Her sunburned cheeks rose with self-satisfaction as she looked up at him. "What're you gonna do? Arrest me?"

"No. I ain't gonna arrest ya."

He walked over to the cottonwood, looked up at its branches, then reached up to pull a long, slender green twig down and jerk it off the low limb it was growing from. Stripping the leaves off the switch, he strode back to Arlis. His temper was flaring, frustration burning. Vaguely, he heard Louis laugh. He grabbed the incredulous Arlis by one arm and shoved her to her knees.

"Hey!" the girl cried in disbelief. "You can't—"

"'Bout time someone did, you snotty little brat. Since your pa ain't here to do it no more, I'm gonna give you the whippin' you deserve for pullin' this goddamn stupid stunt."

Longarm dropped to one knee and hauled the girl across his right thigh extended straight out in front of his belly. She fought him, but her strength was nothing against his. Clamping one hand against the back of her neck, he shoved her head toward the ground, rolling her taut, round, trouser-clad ass up before him. Her hat fell off, her hair brushing the dust. Longarm smacked the switch across her rump three times quickly, the cracks echoing off the near slopes.

Louis laughed.

"That looks like fun," Esmeralda said. "Can I be next?"

Arlis cursed and yelped with each crack of Longarm's switch.

He let the switch hang to the ground but kept his other hand clamped to the back of her neck, holding her head down. "Now, you gonna ride on back to the Cross Fire?"

"No!"

Longarm was about to lay into the taut rump once more, but she somehow suddenly managed to fling herself off his knee, landing in the dust and glaring up at him from her elbows. "There's men back there, you damn fool! Men just like them in the Hope Springs Saloon!"

Longarm scowled. "What men?"

"Take a look, fool!"

Longarm lifted his gaze to follow her pointing finger. Three mares' tails of dust rose along their back trail. Beneath the dust were three riders. Two wore crisscrossed bandoliers on their chests, and the cartridges flashed brassily in the afternoon sun. Longarm stood slowly and dropped the switch.

"You get a look at 'em?"

"No." Arlis stood then, too, brushing dust from her pants and pouting. "But this country is pret' near full to explodin' with nasty varmints of every stripe."

Longarm kept his eyes on the three men who were a hundred yards away and closing at spanking trots, their heads bobbing beneath the tan dust clouds they trailed behind them. "That's why I wanted you to go home, you stubborn cuss."

Arlis was staring red-faced at Longarm. Her white teeth shone between peeled back lips. Her voice was barely louder than a whisper. "I'm gonna watch Del Sager die, damn you."

"If you live that long."

"Here he comes," Little Louis said, chuckling as he stared out at the three approaching riders. "Sure as cat-fights in a brothel, my big brother's come to save me from the big, tough lawdog."

Longarm stared down the powdery trail between the blazing white buttes. "I don't think so, Louis." He swung around and walked back over to his horse tied with the other two where the water hole dribbled off down a slight incline. Shucking his Winchester from the saddle boot, he racked a shell into the chamber and off-cocked the hammer. He walked back out to where Arlis stood, tensely watching the riders approach from fifty yards away.

"What're you gonna do?" she said, a frightened trem-ble in her voice. "What if it's Sager?"

Chapter 13

Longarm stood in the trail with his feet spread, rifle resting casually on his right shoulder. He fished a half-smoked cheroot from his shirt pocket and stuck it between his teeth. "It ain't Sager. No better'n Sager, but no worse. And, fortunately, there's only three."

Arlis looked across her left shoulder at Longarm, curiosity now mixing with the fear in her eyes.

"Go on back and sit on that rock under the cottonwood yonder," Longarm said.

Arlis stood frozen, frowning up at him.

"Go on!"

She jerked into motion, and strode off past Little Louis and toward the shade beneath the cottonwood. She was dropping slowly onto the rock beneath the tree when the three riders rode up to within ten yards of Longarm, tack squawking, bridle chains rattling, sweat-silver horses blowing and snorting. The middle rider grinned and brushed a gloved hand across one of the two cedar-gripped pistols he wore in the cross-draw position from shoulder holsters, the worn brown holsters caressing the crisscrossed bandoliers on his chest.

"Well, I'll be goddamned," he said, showing crooked teeth under a sun-bleached blond mustache half-shaded by a shabby straw sombrero. "If it ain't ole Custis Long his ownself."

"Well, well—if ain't ole Spider Hicks, his ownself. Haven't seen you in a while. How's bounty huntin' been treatin' you?"

Spider Hicks's pale blue eyes were drifting around to the other three behind Longarm, lingering with interest on the women. "I ain't complainin'," he said. "Wouldn't do me much good, even if I wanted to, would it?"

"See you found you some new friends," Longarm said, sliding his gaze to the men on either side of the blond, pale-eyed bounty hunter in the shabby sombrero.

"Yeah, well, my other two buds done give up their ghosts in Bannack, up Montana way. It gets lonely ridin' alone, don't ya know, so I threw in with Pancho Arguello"—he glanced at the man on his left and, in turn, the man on his right—"and 'Three Thumbs' Charlie Payson."

"Don't worry," Payson said, pulling down his mouth corners and holding up both his hands to show he had only one thumb on each. "I got two thumbs just like everyone else. A whore down in Abilene started callin' me that. She said I was so good with my hands when I entertained her south o' the border—if you know what I mean—that it was like I was all thumbs. In a good way." Payson grinned. He had yellow eyes and oddly pale yellow lips, while the rest of his craggy face was nearly as dark as an Indian's.

Longarm rolled his cigar from one side of his mouth to the other and looked at the Mexican to Hicks's left. He was a tall man in a torn charro jacket, with long, black hair hanging straight down from a flat-brimmed hat much like Longarm's but with two bullet holes in the brim. He had two gunnysacks thrown across his saddle pommel, the twisted ends connected by a frayed rope. Whatever was in the sacks—and Longarm thought he knew—owned the shape of pumpkins. And the blood from the pumpkinlike objects had soaked through the burlap of the sacks they were riding in.

"Looks like you been doin' all right for yourselves," the lawman observed.

The Mexican smiled. He was missing both his front teeth.

Hicks smiled, as well, and leaned forward on his saddle horn. "Roland and Lonny Parks done come to bitter ends, Longarm. That's a thousand dollars right there— five hundred per head. Found 'em in the Crystal Buttes just west of Hope Springs. Drunker'n skunks. I'd like to say they give us quite the battle, but, hell, we was practically able to lop their heads off without 'em even rousin' from their blanket rolls!"

"Well, I reckon I'm right obliged."

"Don't mention it." Hicks's scrutinizing gaze had left the women for now and settled on Little Louis Estevez. "Say, who you got there?"

Louis glanced at the three bounty hunters, then lowered his head so his hat hid his face.

"No one special."

"No one special?" Three Thumbs Payson was rising in his stirrups and canting his head around to get a look at Longarm's male prisoner, who kept his head down like a Spanish peon with an adobe wall behind him. "Hell, if that ain't Little Louis Estevez, I don't got eyes to see, and I don't have the paper on him right here in my back pocket!"

"No shit." While Three Thumbs dug into his hip pocket, Hicks looked at Longarm. "Did you really lasso Little Louis?"

"That's none of your concern, Spider." Longarm narrowed his eyes and opened and closed his right hand on his Winchester's receiver, a subtle threat.

"Sure enough!" Three Thumbs flipped open the folded piece of paper he'd removed from his pocket and held it out in front of him for all to see. The wind whipped it this way and that. "It's Little Louis, all right. And he's got three thousand dollars on his ugly, little head!"

"Longarm!" Little Louis cried, casting a terrified gaze at the lawman facing the three bounty hunters.

"Don't worry," Longarm said, keeping his eyes on Hicks, Three Thumbs, and Arguello. "I ain't gonna let 'em saw your head off, Louis." He locked gazes with Hicks. "Be seein' you fellas."

"Ah, come on, Longarm." Hicks dismounted his cream barb and led the horse over to the water hole, speaking over his shoulder. "Let's deal. You let us cut his head off to haul back to Cheyenne, where he's wanted for killin' them lawmen and rustlin' and robbin' trains. Shit! Nobody cares if he's dead or alive. Hell, alive he's more trouble than he's worth. We just need his head!"

Hicks dropped his horse's reins and then, still watching Longarm, walked up to slip the barb's bit from its mouth so the horse could drink. The two shoulder pistols flashed in the sun, as did the bone handle of the big bowie sheathed in a beaded deerskin sheath on his right hip. "We'll split the reward with you four ways. Let's see, one-fourth of three-thousand is . . ."

Longarm turned sideways so that he could keep Hicks and his two partners in clear view. "Like I said— we'll be seein' you fellas. You take all the water you want, rest your weary selves as well as your horses. Until I've ridden out of here with my prisoners, heads attached to their shoulders, I'd like you, Spider, to go stand over there with your pards."

"What for?"

"So I don't get back-shot."

"Longarm, I'd never shoot a federal lawman in the back!"

"Just the same . . ." Longarm lowered his Winchester from his shoulder and aimed it one-handed at the big, blond bounty hunter standing with his barb by the water hole.

Acting like a schoolboy wrongly accused of planting a bullfrog in his teacher's desk, Hicks left his mount and walked back over to where his two partners sat their horses. Longarm kept his Winchester on the three bounty hunters while Arlis fetched her horse. Finally, keeping one eye on the bounty hunters who stood or sat astride their mounts looking bored and faintly exasperated, Longarm got both his prisoners back on their horses.

He mounted his own gray, and then he and Arlis and Little Louis and Esmeralda pulled out. Longarm stayed twisted around in his saddle, keeping all three bounty hunters in plain sight until the shoulder of a butte blocked his view.

"Thanks, Longarm," Louis said when they'd put the water hole a good two hundred yards behind them. The gopher-faced outlaw cast a wary glance behind. "I heard them fellas, just for kicks and giggles, cut men's heads off while they're still alive. A damn grizzly occupation, bounty huntin', if you ask me!"

"I didn't ask you," Longarm said, nonplussed not only about having Arlis Pine riding with him now, but about having three bounty hunters trailing the prisoner he intended to use to lure Del Sager into his trap. Lousy luck. But what did he expect out here?

Arlis kicked her dun up off his right stirrup. "So I reckon you can see why I can't go back—right, Longarm? I'd be easy pickin's with men like that about."

"Arlis?" Longarm kept his head facing forward, stewing. "I'd like you to shut up, too, before I take another switch after your annoying little ass."

"Oh, no, you won't!"

"You can pound my ass, big man." Riding behind Longarm, Esmeralda smiled. "Anytime you like."

Little Louis curled his upper lip at her and cast another fearful glance along their back trail.

The Lone Pine relay station was run by a snaggle-toothed old squaw dog named Percy Blanchard. He and his squaw and two beefy, sullen sons ran the place. When Longarm told Blanchard about what had happened at the next station, Blanchard sent one of his sons up to man the place until the company that owned the line could hire another attendant.

Since there were a few hours of light left, Longarm stopped his crew at Lone Pine only for water and a quick meal of antelope stew and biscuits soaked in stew gravy, with green beans from an airtight tin. Blanchard's squaw, who had one wandering eye that she'd passed on to one of her big, quiet sons, was a good cook. Longarm, Arlis, Little Louis, and Esmeralda—the two prisoners handcuffed together and watched closely by Longarm and his Winchester—ate hungrily while Blanchard tended their horses.

When Longarm's crew was finished eating, the lawman took a few quick puffs off a cheroot while he studied their back trail from the top rail in the holding corral. No sign of Spider Hicks. But he was back there, all right. Most likely laying around waiting for the right time to bushwhack Longarm and take his prisoner and both women. With any luck, Del Sager would ride up on Hicks's bunch and they'd distract one another long enough for Longarm to get his prisoners to Dry Fork.

With any luck . . .

Longarm preferred to take Sager in alive so the killer could hang in front of a cheering crowd for his sins back in Lightning Flat. Despite her conniving, Arlis deserved that much satisfaction. But now all Longarm really cared about was keeping the girl alive and bringing Del Sager's bunch down any way he could, even if that meant letting Spider Hicks take a potshot at the murdering bastard somewhere along Longarm's back trail.

Longarm had traded his crew's spent horses for fresh ones out of Blanchard's remuda, promising the man that Uncle Sam would reimburse him. Blanchard had reluctantly agreed, and now he led the four fresh horses out

of his log barn, a wad of chaw bulging his cheek. Longarm got Little Louis and Esmeralda tied to their saddles,
and then he and Arlis mounted up on their own fresh
mounts.

"You'll likely be seeing at least two more sets of riders," Longarm told Blanchard, sliding his Winchester
into his saddle boot. "I'd more than appreciate it, Percy,
if you didn't swap horses with 'em. Company policy,
maybe—that sorta thing."

"It is company policy," Blanchard growled and stomped
back toward his cabin, where his squaw was sweeping
off the brush-roofed stoop.

Longarm stuffed his cheroot back into his pocket and
ground heels against his gelding's flanks, leading his
prisoners' horses, Arlis riding along behind and still looking pouty after the switching Longarm had given her.
They angled north and east through rolling hills that
aproned the Bear Lodge Mountains rising cool and blue
in the northwest. This was gulley-cut country with scrub
cottonwoods fluttering in the brush-choked ravines and a
smattering of cedar and juniper at the higher elevations.

The sun dropped gradually behind the Bear Lodge
range, painting the dust of Longarm's group gold, then
pink and then dark brown. When the country was more
darkness than light, and the still air acquired an autum-
nal chill, Longarm led them into the deep slash of a canyon rimmed with boulders and pine. At the bottom was
a spring-fed stream sheathed in old cottonwood and a
smattering of aspen and box elder.

Longarm halted his group on a level shelf about thirty
yards up from the stream. Here was good cover in the
form of boulders and brittle shrubs, and a sandstone

ridge wall for a backdrop. He'd just gotten Little Louis and Esmeralda hauled out of their saddles and leading them off toward the base of the ridge, when a voice said behind, "Hi there, little sweety."

Longarm whipped around to see a short, fat man in a long, greasy duck coat and with little brown pig eyes under a floppy-brimmed hat looking at Arlis, who'd just started unsaddling her horse. He held an old Spencer repeating rifle in both hands, the barrel aimed toward Longarm. In the periphery of Longarm's vision, he saw another figure, heard the rasp of a cocking lever, and threw himself sideways as a bullet ripped the air where he'd been standing, sounding like tearing canvas and hammering a boulder with a loud *wham!*, causing all the horses to jump.

The rifle's thunder echoed.

Longarm rolled off his right shoulder, snaking his .44 out of its holster. Automatically, his eyes found the figure standing atop rock rubble that had spilled down from a funnel in the sandstone wall. The Colt roared and flashed brightly in the dense evening shadows.

The man groaned and dropped his head as his knees buckled. The rifle hit the rubble and began sliding down toward the canyon floor. The man followed it, turning somersaults.

Longarm rolled instinctively to his left as another bullet plowed up sand and gravel behind him. He aimed quickly at the fat, squat man near Arlis. The .44 barked three times in quick succession and sent the fat man screaming and throwing the Spencer into the air as he flew straight back off the shelf and into the deeper canyon, where the river coursed.

There was the clack of boots on rock, and Longarm whipped back to his left just as Little Louis dove atop the carbine the first man had lost.

Esmeralda screamed, "*Mierda*—stop, fool!"

The outlaw's hands were not yet cuffed. He grunted and spat saliva between his fluttering lips as he rolled back toward the ridge wall, bringing the carbine up from a shoulder. Longarm aimed at the little man's left arm, intending only to wing him. But Little Louis jerked his face slightly left. Longarm's .44 slug hammered through his left eye, exiting the back of his skull and blowing dust and rock shards from the stone wall behind him.

Louis dropped the carbine as his head slammed against the wall, his left eye socket a puddle of red viscera. His right eye fluttered. Esmeralda screamed, "Louis, you stupid fucker!" as the gopher-faced outlaw's head slid slowly down the rock wall to the ground, leaving a broad, arcing smear of dark red blood and white brain and bone matter on the wall behind him.

His boots jerked. His arms jerked. He lay still in a twisted heap.

Chapter 14

"Shit!" Longarm opened his Colt's loading gate, raised the gun, and turned the cylinder, the empty bullet casings pinging on the rocks around his boots.

Esmeralda stood off to his left, her hands clamped to the sides of her head, holding her hair up like twin black horns as she stared in shock at her dead husband-to-be. Arlis was hunkered on her haunches near her fiddle-footing horse, holding her hands in much the same position as Esmeralda's. She was shuttling her exasperated gaze between the two dead men at the bottom of the ridge. Slowly, she turned her eyes toward where the fat man had been standing before Longarm had blown him into the river gorge.

"Who . . . ?"

"Trail wolves," Longarm grunted. "Common as coyotes around here. Probably wore their horses out bein' chased by a posse and were after ours."

It looked like, given the chance, they would have

helped themselves to the women, as well. By the looks on both Arlis and Esmeralda's faces, the women were well aware of that.

Longarm looked around cautiously, as there could be more from the same lair these two hailed from. But when he stood at the lip of the steep slope angling off toward the river sliding in the gorge below, he saw only the fat man sprawled at the bottom of the incline, on his back, one leg curled beneath the other, his head turned sharply to one side. Blood glistened from a corner of his grimacing mouth in the fading light.

Esmeralda walked over to Little Louis and shook her head slowly as she stared down at the dead outlaw. Longarm followed her and picked up the rifle Louis had been going for, but Esmeralda appeared to be in no mood to make a play for it. With a fateful sigh, she plopped down a rock beside her dead beau, dropped elbows to knees, and pooched her lips out as she looked wryly up at Longarm.

"Well, now what are you going to do, lawman? How are you going to go fishing without bait?"

Longarm tossed a pair of handcuffs at her feet. "Put those on one of your wrists. Lock the other one around that root there." He indicated an old, dried cedar root angling up out of the ground before disappearing under a boulder near Louis. "Good and tight."

Esmeralda sighed again, but, shocked and weary, she did as ordered.

Longarm turned to Arlis, who was still hunkered down, hands clamped to the sides of her head. The pluck that had brought her out here appeared gone. Now she just looked like a very frightened girl who was wondering what in hell had ever possessed her to leave her ranch.

She needed something to do, something to think about besides the carnage before her. "Can you unrig all the horses and lead 'em down to the river?"

She swallowed, drew a ragged breath. She rose and began unsaddling the four horses.

Longarm holstered his Colt, then went over and grabbed the ankles of the bushwhacker lying dead near Louis. Without ceremony, he flung the body down the slope and watched it roll, limbs flopping, loosing little rock- and-sand slides behind it before it piled up about ten feet to the right of the dead fat man. That done, Longarm retrieved his saddlebags containing his cooking gear and began forming a fire ring with rocks. He glanced at the green sky fading toward turquoise. Not much light left. He needed to get a fire going and make coffee before good dark.

"What about my friend here?"

Longarm looked at Esmeralda who sat on her rock, leaning forward with her elbows on her knees. She canted her head toward Louis. The outlaw was on his side, staring in the general direction of Longarm, one-eyed.

Longarm studied the Mexican whore for a stretched moment, then rose and walked over, digging his handcuff key from his pants pocket. She frowned at him curiously as he shoved the key into the lock on her handcuff, opened it with a ratcheting click.

"Cover him. But leave him here. I want his brother to find him."

Rubbing her freed wrist, she studied Longarm in the failing light.

"You're free to go," he grunted, heading back over to the fire ring. "I got no time for you. Go or stay—it's up to you. Just don't give me any trouble, or you'll end up like him."

She brushed her hair back from her face. "How do you know I will not wait for Sager, lead him to you? He's not going to like it now—you killing his brother."

"Lady, I wish you would."

As Longarm gathered tinder and kindling, and Arlis led the horses down a game trail into the river gorge, Esmeralda strode thoughtfully over to her gear piled up on the ground where Louis's horse had been standing and gathered his soogan. She removed the rawhide ties and carried it over to Louis, then crouched over the dead outlaw as she flung the blanket out across him.

With a sigh, she straightened, looking down at the blanket-covered carcass. "Good-bye, Louis. You weren't much of a man, but you treated me well until you saw the lawman's little bitch. For that, I give you *this*!" She brought her right boot back and flung it forward hard, causing the bundle to jerk. "*Bastardo!* Probably wouldn't have married me, anyway . . ."

Longarm got the coffee going. As he did, Esmeralda gathered her own gear across the fledging fire from him, then kicked out of her boots.

"I'm going for a swim," she said, unbuttoning her shirt. She smiled, her hair flopping around her shoulders. "Want to come?"

"Nah, I'm good."

"Sure?" With a flourish, she removed her shirt, let it drop at her feet. "It could be fun."

Longarm grinned and leaned back on an elbow. He had to hand it to her—she wasted no time. Her man was dead, and she'd need another one soon. Young women didn't last long alone. "I'm sure it would. You go ahead. Have a good time. Me—it's been a long ride, and I'm beat."

She stripped down to just her camisole and stocking feet. Breasts swaying behind the wash-worn undergarment, she grabbed a grubby towel from her saddlebags and flung her hair out as she whipped around and headed for the game trail. She disappeared down the slope, and Longarm could hear her the gravel tumbling behind her as she made her way down the incline.

He'd bought some jerked rabbit, a tin of peaches, half a loaf of crusty brown bread, and cheese from Blanchard's wife. He set the food out on a flat rock and sat back, crossing his ankles near the fire and listening to the coffeepot chug and sputter, nibbling the jerky while keeping his eyes on his back trail. More than watching, he listened. It was a quiet night, and he'd hear riders approaching from a half mile away.

He'd had one cup of coffee when he realized he was feeling edgy about something besides Del Sager. Arlis hadn't returned from the stream. Neither had Esmeralda. The sky was damn near black, two stars winking clearly straight above the northern ridge.

He set the coffeepot on a rock beside the snapping, foot-high flames, and took the game path that Esmeralda had taken into the gorge. On the still air he could smell the horses, and he followed their scent to where Arlis had picketed them to a short rope strung between two cottonwoods. The horses appeared content as they stood, heads and tails drooping, but there was no sign of either Arlis or the Mexican.

Quietly, his hand draped over his pistol butt, Longarm stole through the brush toward the creek, the trees standing dark around him. The river was a dark brown blanket beyond, flashing as though trimmed in dull silver sequins.

A girl's laughter, like a small wind chime, carried through the still air.

Longarm stopped.

Water splashed, sounding like an even smaller chime nudged by a vagrant breeze.

Lines cutting across his freshly wind- and sunburned forehead, Longarm continued walking. He stopped at the edge of the narrow, deep stream. The lines in his forehead cut deeper when he saw the silhouettes of two figures on the other side of the stream. One sat on the opposite back, her back to the ridge wall that rose like a velvet blanket canvas behind her. The other was in the stream, her head with long, black hair glistening wetly down her dark brown back in the ambient light, even with Arlis's belly.

There were wet sucking sounds mingling with those of the stream lapping gently against its banks. Arlis had her own head thrown back as she leaned back on her arms. She sighed and groaned softly, occasionally waggling her spread knees, between which Esmeralda's head bobbed and turned slightly from side to side.

When it dawned on Longarm that the two were engaged in carnal frolic, his ears turned hot. He wanted to turn away, but something about the vision of the two female silhouettes together on the other side of the spring-fed stream, and the mesmerizing light of the canyon—the dark, cool air seemed to be raining little nuggets of quicksilver—prevented him from doing so. It was almost as though he'd fallen fallen asleep and tumbled into an erotic dream.

Someone sighed, the sound cutting clearly across the water. Longarm saw that Arlis had straightened her back. Esmeralda lifted her head and turned toward him.

"Oh, uh . . . sorry."

He started to turn away.

Esmeralda said, chuckling, "Hold your horses, lawman."

She turned away from Arlis and waded toward him across the stream. She was wet and brown and speckled lime from the trees and silver from the air, her black hair hanging like a mantilla behind her shoulders. Arlis followed her, her own skin golden, her hair hanging messily about her cheeks. She raised her slender arms, running her fingertips across the water. Her nipples dragged across the surface of the slowly sliding stream.

As both girls climbed up the bank, Longarm became aware of his enormous hard-on pressing painfully against his pants. He wanted to turn away—he had no time for a waking dream, with Del Sager bearing down on him—but his feet had turned to concrete. They were two forest sprites walking toward him, one dark and bosomed, full womanly hips swaying as she moved; the other, slighter, fairer, breasts smaller but little pink nipples hard as sewing thimbles. Water dripped off them both.

Bare feet crackled over grass and last year's fallen leaves.

Longarm stood mesmerized, his throat tight, heart pounding insistently. Esmeralda stopped in front of him, the tips of her large, full breasts brushing against his shirt. He could feel the heat of her behind the coolness from the water. She smelled musky, sweet.

"You want both of us?" she whispered.

Before he could answer, she kissed him quickly, poking her tongue into his mouth and then withdrawing it just as quickly and dropping to her knees. He felt no fear when she started to unbuckle his cartridge belt. He and they were on another plane here, far from the three men he'd just killed.

Far from Del Sager.

As his cartridge belt dropped to his feet and Esmeralda began digging into the fly of his pants, her hand hungry, desperate, Arlis stood to Esmeralda's left. She rose up on the tips of her bare toes, placed his hand on one of her breasts, and closed her mouth over his.

A warm, soft, lingering kiss.

As she caressed his tongue with her own, he tasted her breath. At the same time, his cock sprang free of its tight confines. The cool air touched it, made him shudder slightly. Then he felt the silky wet warmth of Esmeralda's mouth closing over the bulging head and sliding down, down the shaft until the head was pressed firmly against the far back of her throat.

After a time—Longarm's knees were growing so weak he was having trouble standing—Arlis pulled away from him. She dropped to her knees beside Esmeralda, who withdrew her mouth from Longarm's cock. As it sprang free of her lips, Arlis reached up and wrapped her warm hand around it, shoving her own head toward Esmeralda. Their two open mouths barely touched. While Arlis opened and closed her hand around Longarm's cock, the two girls nibbled each other's lips, touched tongues, fondled breasts.

All the while they sighed and groaned and gave little alluring, animal grunts.

Longarm gritted his teeth against the girl's caress.

Finally, they each took turns kissing and nuzzling his cock while they fondled each other, nuzzled each other's breasts.

Longarm ground his heels into the dirt, ground his teeth.

Finally, he stumbled backwards and dropped to his ass with a grunt.

The girls laughed.

Esmeralda crouched over him and ran her tongue along the side of his iron-hard shaft, then looked at Arlis.

"Who gets this big rod in her pussy first?"

"Draw straws?"

Esmeralda shrugged. She found two dried grass stems. While Arlis continued to gently pump Longarm's cock with one hand, causing blood to hammer against his eardrums, she drew a stem with her other. It was the short one.

Esmeralda laughed huskily, climbed on top of Longarm, straddling him, and impaled herself hard and deep. She rode him with reckless abandon while Arlis took turns kissing Longarm and nibbling Esmeralda's nipples.

When he'd finished fucking Esmeralda, both girls nuzzled him back to life. Then he took Arlis in the missionary position while Esmeralda, sprawled with her breasts sloping against the grass, soothed Arlis's love cries with gentle kisses while smoothing her sweat-damp hair back from her temples.

Arlis ground her heels into Longarm's butt when she came, mewling like a mare.

Later, they gathered their clothes and returned to the camp to eat hungrily, sipping coffee laced with whiskey. They sat around the fire in postcoital silence, listening to the coyotes. When Longarm woke early the next morning under his soogan blankets, he found himself spooned against Arlis while Esmeralda's full naked breasts pressed against his back, her face buried in his neck.

She was snoring softly, her breath warm against his ear.

His arms were curled around Arlis, his hands on her breasts. He was hard as a rock.

In the hour before dawn, both girls quietly, dutifully relieved him of his burden.

Chapter 15

Skull Butte relay station hunkered low in a broad canyon, the round-topped butte it had been named for bathed in the soft, cool light of mid-morning.

The butte jutted at the east end of the yard. Lower buttes surrounded the place, which, made up of sod-roofed mud shacks and ramshackle sheds, fenced haystacks, and corrals equipped with dipping and dehorning chutes, appeared to have been a small ranch headquarters at one time. Whoever had owned the ranch had likely decided a few years ago that working for a stage line would be more profitable than running cattle on these dry hills crusted with sage and cactus, and where Indians and non-Indian outlaws likely ran wild as the wolves.

Longarm led Arlis and Esmeralda, who rode with her hands free now and who had chosen to tag along with the lawman and Arlis rather than go it alone in this woolly country, down the curving two-track trail and into the yard. It was a rundown place, with mud swallows building their cone-shaped nests under the eaves of the long bunkhouse, their wings flashing green in the buttery light. Horses milling in the corrals told Longarm it was occupied, though.

The house was off to the left, near a springhouse and a privy that leaned to the southeast. There were curtains over the windows, but a pallid tendril of smoke curled from the mud brick chimney. The finely churned dust of the yard was scored by fresh-shod hoofprints.

"Hello the house," Longarm said in nearly his normal voice. It was so morning-quiet, despite the squealing of the swallows, that he could have been heard in the privy fifty yards away.

The scarred gray door, shaded by the brush arbor, stayed closed. No movement in the dusty, dark windows fronting the closed flour-sack curtains. A couple of horses blew in the corral on the other side of the yard, one scraping a hip on the snubbing post. Longarm was about to call again when, looking around, he saw a stand of cottonwoods lining a creek running along the base of the yucca-spiked bluffs to the south. Something was moving among the trees.

Flicking the keeper thong free of his .44, he said, "You two stay here."

He touched heels to his dun's flanks and rode straight on across the yard, past two small fenced areas containing low mounds of hay and straw, around a tumbledown corral, and into the cool shade of the faintly rustling cottonwoods. Twenty yards from the creek, he reined up suddenly and slipped the Colt from its holster.

A pucker of apprehension drew his brows together as he stared at three men hanging from a stout, low branch of a large cottonwood, half of whose branches hung over the muddy brown creek. Spider Hicks, Pancho Arguello, and Three Thumbs Charlie Payson hung from a branch on the tree's other side, their feet only about two feet off the ground. From nooses looped over the branch above their heads, then tied off lower down on the other side of the trunk, they twisted slowly this way and that, making the rope creak faintly.

Spider Hicks's neck had been stretched a good eight inches, and his tongue hung curled from the right corner of his pain-twisted mouth. Arguello's eyes were wide open and staring horrifically. He'd kicked out of one of his boots, which lay on the ground beneath him, and half out of the other one, made of hand-tooled Mexican cowhide decorated with little red rose petals.

Three Thumbs' chin was dipped to his chest, and he almost seemed to be grinning.

Longarm looked around quickly, his heart thudding. He saw Hicks's cream barb casually cropping bluestem on the other side of the creek. Otherwise, there was nothing, no one out here but dead men. The horse switched its tail, gave Longarm a faintly interested look, and lowered its head once more to the grass.

Longarm was glancing at the ground, where deep scuff marks showed where the bounty hunters had been dragged, kicking and screaming, off to the hang tree. He turned the dun around several times, looking around, trying to get a count of the number of horses that had been out here. Too tough to tell among all the boot and hoof prints.

Arlis's voice called, "Longarm!"

He whipped his head around. The two girls sat their

horses where he'd left them, only now they were turned toward the main house. A man was moving down off the gallery, holding a rifle. He was moving slowly, holding his rifle in both hands. Longarm shoved his heels into the dun's flanks and galloped back into the yard, rocking his .44's hammer back loudly and aiming at the man with the rifle.

"Hold it! Drop the rifle, mister!"

The man was tall and thin, wasted-looking, with his long face craggy as weathered sandstone, and spindly shoulders that appeared perpetually hunched. He looked around warily, dark-blue eyes winking in the sun. He licked his lips several times, then lifted his gaze to regard Longarm aiming the pistol at him from atop the dun.

From the wary look in the man's eyes, and the way his hands shook, he seemed to be half in shock.

"Easy, amigo," Longarm said. "Set the rifle down, and we'll talk. We mean no harm."

The man curled his lip and narrowed an eye. "You the federal?"

"That's right."

The man nodded thoughtfully. He removed one hand from his rifle and lowered the barrel, holding on to the old Springfield by its rear stock that was held together with rusty wire and shrunk rawhide. Longarm looked at the man's shaking hands once more.

"Who decorated your tree for you, friend?"

"Said his name was Sager."

"Sager!" Arlis exclaimed, looking both frightened and angry as she whipped head toward the cottonwoods.

Longarm looked around cautiously. As he did, he

slowly returned his pistol to its cross-draw holster, leaving the keeper thong free, then reached down and slid his Winchester from the saddle boot. "How long ago he do the decoratin'?"

"Way early this mornin'. Got me out of bed. They had them three fellas tied belly down over their saddles. I didn't watch what they was doin' back there—they told me to stay out of the way and to tell the next man through here—they was expectin' you, sure enough—that you were gonna die slow and painful for what you did to . . ."

The skin above the bridge of the man's long nose wrinkled thoughtfully.

"Little Louis?"

"Yeah. Little Louis. They said you'd be a federal lawdog. I could hear them hangin' those boys, but I didn't look. The screamin' and fightin' was awful. When they rode out, they told me to leave 'em hangin' or I'd join 'em." The gray-haired man shook his head. "Awful thing—listenin' to them men chokin' and coughin' and beggin' for help, and there weren't nothin' I could do. I just went on inside and put my head down on the table."

Longarm and the girls were all looking around. Longarm felt a creeping sensation between his shoulders, as though a target had been drawn there and sites were being arranged on it. "You know where they went?"

"Nope. They said they just wanted to give you and whoever's ridin' with ya somethin' to think about. They'd be meetin' up with you right soon."

"*Sí*," said Esmeralda thinly. She swallowed. "I for one am thinking about it. *Mierda*."

Arlis looked at Longarm, her cheeks pale and hollow. "How'd they get in front of us?"

"Probably took a shortcut from wherever they came from. Knew I'd be heading east with my prisoner." Longarm quietly racked a shell into his rifle's chamber, though there was no need to be quiet. The feeling between his shoulders told him Sager not only knew he'd arrived at the relay station but was watching every move he made. "You two go on into the station. Leave your horses here."

Arlis and Esmeralda both looked as though that was just what they'd been waiting to be told. Without hesitation, both girls swung down from their saddles and headed for the house, looking around warily as they climbed the two rotten gallery steps and headed on inside. Esmeralda poked her dark head back out, looking around, the dry breeze tusseling her hair.

Longarm swung down from his own horse. He glanced at the man with the long, gray hair and the palsy. "Who're you?"

"Luke Jackson."

"I'm Custis Long. Call me Longarm." Longarm gathered up the reins of all three horses, and, keeping his rifle butt snugged against his cartridge belt, his right index finger curled through the trigger guard, he began leading the horses toward the main corral, directly across the yard from the house. "How many riders were with Sager?"

Jackson stood tensely in front of his stoop, fingering his chin and looking around, closing first one eye, then the other. "Three. Bad-looking sonso'bitches. Merciless bastards."

Longarm lifted the latching wire over the corral post, kicked the bottom wire free of the gate, and drew the gate open on its hide-and-metal hinges. It sagged into the arcing furrow it had carved into the yard. Longarm glanced around again warily, expecting a bullet at any time, then led the three horses into the corral.

He figured the three bounty hunters led by Hicks had found Little Louis. In turn, Sager had found them with his dead brother. Since Sager had already been told about the federal lawman who'd taken down Louis, it probably hadn't been hard for Hicks, Payson, and Arguello to convince him they weren't responsible for the gopher-faced outlaw's demise. Sager had killed the men just the same.

As a grisly promise to Longarm . . .

If Sager had only three other men with him, he might be waiting for more before he made his move. He knew Longarm's reputation and probably wanted as many men siding him as he had in his gang, before he tried blowing the wick of the federal lawman who'd killed his little brother. Also, the more men Sager had, the easier it would be for him to take Longarm alive so he could torture him slow.

Meanwhile, Sager's men would likely have a good time with Arlis and Esmeralda.

Jackson licked his lips as he walked into the corral, pulling the gate closed behind him. "This is an awful mess you're in, mister. I done heard of Del Sager before. Wouldn't wanna meet him again . . . but I got a feelin' I'm gonna."

Longarm was unsaddling his dun. Jackson leaned his rifle against the barn's log wall and began uncinching the latigo of Esmeralda's bay, an awkward maneuver with his shaking hands. With one eye, Longarm scanned the ridges around him. "What's the best high ground for keeping an eye on the station?"

"I'd say up there." Jackson pointed toward Skull Butte. "See that notch near the top. Sager's probably got someone layin' up there with a spyglass. Maybe a rifle. Too far for accurate shooting, but they could signal someone down here."

Longarm considered the information.

"You alone out here, Jackson?"

The man sighed as he stripped off Esmeralda's saddle. "'Fraid so. And I ain't much help with a rifle, neither. Bursitis of the shoulder. Been the shits around here since my wife died seven years ago from bad water, and my son was killed two years ago in a raid by Southern Cheyenne. Just me since then. Turned my place over to the stage line last summer." He sighed again. "Yep . . . just me, I'm afraid."

"You don't mind if I exchange these three mounts for fresh ones, do you? They came from Blanchard."

"Help yourself, but I only got two saddle ponies. Them two there." He pointed to a paint and a sorrel standing head to head on the corral's far side. "The rest are pullers."

"Later." Longarm heaved Arlis's saddle over the top of the corral. He wanted to get a better lay of the land before he decided how he'd proceed. The situation would be a whole lot less complicated without the girls. He bet both were wishing like hell they'd made other decisions. Too late now. They were all stuck with one another. And Longarm had no idea how he was going to do his job, as in taking down Del Sager, when he was hamstrung with two females.

"Yeah, later," he said, holding his rifle and taking a three-hundred-and-sixty-degree look around the chalky ridges. "Let's see what Sager's next move is. Might just forget the horses and take off on foot."

"You don't mind if we head back to the house now, do you?" Jackson's voice was raspy, tremulous. "Bein' out here's makin' me a little nervy, if it's all the same to you."

"I've felt better myself." Longarm saw that there was hay in the crib and water in the troughs, so he ducked through the corral slats and began heading toward the house, turning full circles with his rifle held high. Jackson hurried along behind him.

Longarm had just planted a foot on the first gallery step, when something rammed into the awning post to his right. Wood slivers peppered his shoulder.

The rifle's bellow echoed behind him.

"Ah, hell!" Jackson screamed as he shouldered the door open and ducked into the house.

Chapter 16

Longarm dashed through the door behind Jackson and slammed it.

He shouldered up to the window right of the door, tossed his hat on the floor, and, peeling the curtain back from the glass with his rifle barrel, edged a look around the frame. The pane was warped and dusty, so he couldn't see much. No one appeared to be moving out there.

"From behind the barn."

Longarm turned to Esmeralda, who stood with her back pressed up against the whitewashed wall beside a window kitty-corner across the room from him. She was holding the rifle she'd taken off the bushwhacker. Her dark eyes reflected the light from the window near Longarm.

"I saw a shadow, some smoke. He's behind the barn."

Arlis stood on the other side of the window from Longarm. Her hazel eyes were glassy with fear. "What're we gonna do?"

Before Longarm could respond, a man called his name. It came from behind the cabin and was just loud enough for Longarm to hear.

"Longarm!" came the yell again, louder. "It's Del Sager!"

There was an outside door at the rear of the lodge, between the kitchen and what passed for a parlor and a sleeping area for overnight stage passengers with several curtained doorways in its far right wall. Jackson stood tensely between the two areas, his eyes flicking wildly toward the lodge's four windows.

"They got us surrounded," he said, breathless.

Longarm brushed past the man. He removed the locking bar over the brackets in the rear door and glanced over his shoulder. "Everyone get down against a wall. Sit tight."

"Longarm!" Sager shouted, his voice pinched with emotion. "You killed my brother, you sonofabitch. Wasn't even him you wanted, was it?"

Longarm flipped the metal latch, drew the door wide, and stepped back to the left side of the frame, holding his cocked rifle up high across his chest. He glanced quickly outside, seeing nothing but scrub brush and trees behind the privy, a low, yucca-crusted bluff seventy or so yards beyond the trees, and a tarp-covered woodpile.

He drew his head back behind the wall. "That's right, Sager. He was the bait. I meant to keep him alive, but he had other ideas!"

"I got other ideas for you, Longarm!"

A rifle exploded twice. Both slugs hammered the outside wall around the door, spewing wood slivers.

Longarm slid his right eye around the frame, peering out.

Sager stood off the corner of an old brick shack, probably an old mining shack and original ranch dwelling. A tall, slender man with a ratty-looking beard that hung to the middle of his chest, he held a Winchester with both hands. He wore a black hat and a long, torn, and weather-stained gray duster. The duster was open to reveal to cartridge belts overlapping on his lean waist.

Sager's full lips stretched a devilish grin. He removed one hand from his Winchester to stretch it straight out to his side, waving.

Longarm gritted his teeth as he stepped into the door's opening, quickly raising his rifle. He fired two quick rounds and then a third. A waste of lead. Sager had stepped back behind the springhouse, and Longarm's slugs only plunked the spindly, dry shrubs around where the outlaw had been standing. One tore mud chunks from the springhouse and screeched as it ricocheted.

"Del Sager!" Arlis shouted as she bounded up from where she'd been sitting and took long, fast strides toward the open door. "I'm going to kill you, you son of a—!"

Two more slugs hammered the outside wall as a third rifle cracked. Arlis screamed and dropped to her knees, dropping her rifle and cupping her hands to her ears. Longarm grabbed the girl's left arm and jerked her back against the wall behind him. She groaned when she plowed into the wall, knocking an airtight tin from a cabinet. Crouching, Longarm lurched into the opening once more and slammed the door closed.

A bullet hammered the outside of it, causing it to leap in its frame. The slug cracked it but did not go through.

"There's the third man," Longarm said half to himself.

He looked out a window beyond Arlis, who sat with her back to the wall, eyes wide as saucers. A slender, dark figure moved near the crest of a cone-crested butte northeast of the house.

Outside, Sager laughed. "You're surrounded, Longarm! Might wanna think about comin' out. You do, we'll think of goin' easy on them two nice-looking pieces of tail you got with you!"

"Fucker!" Arlis grated out, turning toward the door and showing her teeth like an enraged dog. "That fucker's gotta die, Longarm. He's just gotta die!"

"Workin' on it. In the meantime, you keep your goddamn head down."

Ignoring Arlis's indignant scowl, Longarm strode, crouching, across the lodge to the front. He glanced at Jackson, who sat with his back to a ceiling joist, his old rifle across his thighs.

"You said there were four here, counting Sager?"

Jackson licked his chapped lips and nodded.

Keeping low, Longarm edged a look above the windowsill, appraising the station yard quickly. He pulled his head down and sat on his butt, back to the wall between the window and the door. Two things were certain—he wouldn't be continuing on to Dry Fork. Sager's men would only run him down. He and the girls couldn't remain here, because the station house was a dangerous trap that he'd walked right into.

He and the girls had to get out of here.

He looked again at Jackson, who was staring at him expectantly, as though trying to read what he was thinking.

"If I wanted to hightail it out of here, take to high, broken country where I might have a chance against seven or eight shooters, what's my best direction?"

Jackson licked his lips again, sleeved the slick sheen of sweat from his brick-red forehead. "Straight east. Over there's the breaks of Skull River."

"All right." Longarm chewed his lip, glancing at Esmeralda and then Arlis. "You two up for a mad dash to the horses when I tell you to run like hell?"

Esmeralda sat with her back to the east wall, rifle across her knees. Her calico blouse had come unbuttoned halfway down her chest, laying bare a fringe of pink camisole and the two cherry-tan inside curves of her ample breasts. Her black hair was mussed, her eyes glistening black disks gleaming through it. "What about the *bastardo* behind the barn?"

"I'm gonna try to send him back to his maker. But I'm gonna need your help." Longarm glanced at Jackson. "I'm gonna need the shooting help of all three of you."

Jackson sighed raggedly. "I'll do what I can."

"*Sí, sí,*" Esmeralda said, nodding. "Anything is better than sitting here waiting to die!"

Ten minutes later, Longarm had positioned Esmeralda by the lodge's back window. He's placed Arlis by the side window, facing the low butte from atop which the third gunman had fired. Now, slowly, he cracked the front door, letting a finger of bright yellow light angle across his boots and one trouser leg as he peered across the yard.

The sun was high, the heat reflecting off the churned dust of the yard. The barn and corrals all looked washed out and pale gray. The horses stood beneath a brush arbor on the far side of the main corral, tan dust rising as a couple stomped around to scratch or to nip at biting flies.

Longarm closed the door and glanced at Jackson. "When I give the word, start shooting at the barn. Keep that bastard behind it. I'm gonna run off to the east and into those cottonwoods, then follow the creek around behind the corral." He turned toward Arlis and Esmeralda, who watched him anxiously. "When I have the shooter back there, I'll give a yell. All three of you come runnin'. I'll cover you while you saddle the horses. Then we'll ride the hell out of here, straight east and into that rough country Jackson told us about."

"Just the three of you against Sager?" the old man said, shaking his head slowly, the dry breeze plucking at his coarse gray hair.

"Don't bet against us, old man," Esmeralda snarled, curling her nostrils. "We three have been through a lot, and we're not finished yet!"

Arlis's cheeks colored slightly and Longarm knew she was remembering their stolen moments of bliss last night by the spring-fed creek.

Longarm said, "Get ready. Don't waste too many shells—five or six shots'll keep 'em pinned down long enough for me to get into the trees. Then bar both doors and keep an eye out to see if any of 'em leaves their cover." He drew the keeper thong across the hammer of his holstered Colt. "Just don't get that eye shot out!"

Arlis nodded. "You got it. I'm just hopin' maybe I can blow Sager's eye out, like you done his brother."

"Nothin' fancy, Arlis," Longarm advised. "Just keep him pinned. We'll nail the son of a bitch later."

He cracked the front door again, peered out.

"Now!"

He bolted out onto the gallery, spun right, and, hoisting off his left hand, leaped over the railing at the far end. As soon as his boots hit the dirt, there was the crash of glass being broken out of the windows with the girls' rifle butts, followed a second later by the din of rifle fire.

Jackson stood in a two-foot gap of the open door, triggering shots toward the barn. Longarm saw the man in the corner of his left eye just as he began sprinting and crouching, straight east across the yard. He stayed in the cover of chokecherry and willow thickets, leaping rocks and swerving around a springhouse.

Behind him the girls and Jackson hammered off about five rounds apiece. The rifles lifted staccato wails followed by the screech of ricocheting lead.

Then Longarm was in the cottonwoods. The stream in its narrow banks was dead ahead. He charged toward it, hearing a couple of Sager's men shouting behind him. A rifle belched three times, the shots spaced about two seconds apart. Whoever was shooting had no target in his sites; he was probably only shooting because he'd glimpsed Longarm's dash toward the creek.

The four killers had thought they had the lawman and the two girls pinned down. They'd likely underestimated the sand in both Arlis and Esmeralda. Those two would do, Longarm vaguely thought as he leaped the creek and dropped down behind a boulder to get the lay of the land.

A rifle barked loudly from somewhere above. A bullet slammed into the top of the rock Longarm had crouched behind. He threw himself back against the cutbank eroded out of the base of a butte. A man was moving down a gravelly trough. He stopped, crouched, and fired. That slug, too, hammered the boulder. He continued running, half-sliding down the trough toward the river and about twenty yards downstream from Longarm.

The lawman raised his Winchester. The shooter, who until now had been unaccounted for, was heading for a jumble of boulders. If he got behind those, he'd be there to stay. Desperately, Longarm led the man on his descent down the trough.

The Winchester roared.

He ejected the spent shell and took hasty aim.

Bam! Bam! Bam! Bam!

The last shot took the legs out from under the running man. He screamed, flew forward, and rolled violently, dropping his rifle, until he piled up with an audible thud against the boulder nest he'd been heading toward. Dust rose. Weakly, the man tried to haul himself up.

Longarm finished him with a slug that puffed dust from his brown brush jacket. He slumped to the ground, and rolled twice more before coming to final rest in a cactus snag.

Crouching down behind the rock again, Longarm thumbed cartridges from his cartridge belt through the Winchester's loading gate. He could smell hot iron, scorched brass, and powder smoke. Seeing no one else around, he moved out from behind the rock and followed a narrow game path along the east side of the stream, paralleling the faintly rippling water. He kept a sharp lookout for the man behind the barn.

That man would have the easiest journey, out of the line of fire from the cabin, toward Longarm. If he hadn't seen Longarm's dash from the cabin, all three men had heard the rifle shots and now knew where he was.

"Billy Lee!"

The voice echoed from ahead and on the other side of the stream. Longarm dove behind a thick patch of brush and heeled low, waiting.

Chapter 17

Longarm heard the Sager rider—not Sager himself but likely the man who'd been shooting at the cabin from behind the barn—moving among the trees on the other side of the faintly gurgling stream. From the sound of the snapping brush, he was roughly twenty yards upstream and just inside the trees.

A twig snapped. Silence.

Then: "Billy Lee!"

Longarm looked around the right side of the snag. It took him nearly a minute to pick out the very edge of a hat brim and about six inches of a rifle barrel poking out from behind a tree near where the bounty hunters hung, twisting slowly. Longarm slowly, quietly levered a shell into his Winchester's breech and drew several deep, calming breaths.

He licked his lower lip and pinched his voice slightly, as though with pain. "*Here!*"

A bearded face edged out from behind the tree. The

entire rifle and half a torso appeared. He was wearing a striped shirt and suspenders, and he had a pistol holstered for the cross-draw on his right hip. Longarm drew a quick bead. The Winchester boomed.

The man disappeared behind the tree. He reappeared a moment later, bounding out from the tree's other side. He ran crouching, stumbling, grunting. He'd lost his hat, and his bearded face was stretched painfully. From his hip, he triggered his Henry repeater. The slug splashed water on Longarm's side of the stream.

The man racked a fresh round, and Longarm, keeping his rifle on the man, narrowing his right eye, held his breath and took up the slack in his trigger finger.

Bang!

"Gawd-*damn*!" the bearded gent said, continuing to stumble toward a bend in the stream, away from Longarm.

Longarm spat a curse and bounded up and out from behind his cover, racking a fresh round into his Winchester's breech. He ran upstream, saw the man barreling headfirst through several young cottonwoods. He was heading for a ravine that angled toward the stream from Longarm's side of it. Red glistened high on his shoulder and around his upper left thigh.

He triggered another wild shot as he ran. Longarm continued to run after him. The man was out of commission, but Longarm wanted them all dead or he'd likely pay for it later.

He drew even with the running shooter, who no longer appeared to have the strength to raise his brass-receivered Henry. The man came on through the trees like a wounded animal, screaming and cursing in desperation. He dropped his rifle and groped for one of his two, ivory-gripped cross-draw pistols.

Longarm stopped on his side of the narrow, shallow stream and snugged his Winchester's barrel against his shoulder. He leveled the sites, let the man move into them.

The man saw Longarm at the same time Longarm drew a bead on his forehead. The man dropped his lower jaw. He had lilac-colored eyes that complemented the pewter of his patchy beard. They widened, glistened.

Another raging scream had just begun to rise from his throat when Longarm's bullet plunked through the man's forehead. The impact stood him straight up and threw him back against a broad-boled box elder. He bounced off the box elder, stumbled forward, tripped over a blown-down tree, and splashed into the stream.

He went under on his back, and rose slowly, blood turning the water around him pale amber. As he lolled in the slow stream, his wide, lilac eyes stared as though in innocent amazement at the cloudless blue sky.

Longarm hightailed it without further trouble over to the main corral.

The horses were milling nervously, two trotting circles around the others, necks and tails arched. The lawman worked his way through the milling beasts—the smell of the hot mounts in the close confines was nearly suffocating—to the front of the corral and looked around the yard. He'd heard a few sporadic shots fired from the cabin, which meant that Arlis, Esmeralda, and Jackson were keeping Sager and the other surviving bushwhacker pinned down somewhere.

That wouldn't last long.

Longarm was feeling downright fortunate, however, that the rest of the outlaw's men had not yet joined him. Maybe they never would. That would be an even bigger bit of good luck. If Sager had only one other man with him, he'd be a hell of a lot easier to kill.

And that was Longarm's intention. He was no vigilante, but he had the girl to worry about, not to mention Jackson, who was another endangered innocent bystander here. Trying to take Sager alive would be too risky. It didn't break Longarm's heart. Plenty of witnesses had seen Sager hang Alvin Pine. The man deserved to die. Without a doubt, he'd hang for his recent transgressions, and there was no point in risking the man breaking free again while he waited for the hangman.

Reasonably certain that the yard between the cabin and the corral was clear, Longarm yelled, "Arlis, Esmeralda— let's go!"

They'd been awaiting the summons. The front door burst open, and the girls bolted out, Arlis in the lead and Esmeralda bringing up the rear. Arlis sprinted across the yard, her rifle in one hand, her hair bouncing on her shoulders. Esmeralda moved more slowly, holding her own rifle in both hands as she turned slow circles to cast her wary gaze around the yard.

When they both had made it to the corral, Longarm didn't need to tell them what to do. While he kept a close watch on the yard, knowing that Jackson was watching from the rear of the main lodge, the girls made fast work of saddling and bridling three fresh horses.

A few shots sounded from the buttes behind the

lodge. Jackson answered with his old blunderbuss. Long-arm heard Sager and the other killer shouting back and forth. Neither knew what was happening, though they'd heard the shooting. They knew something was happening but were likely hesitant, maybe even afraid, to storm the lodge and risk walking into a trap. Longarm felt a keen satisfaction having turned the tables on the killers. He just hoped it didn't backfire, in turn, on him. If Sager's other men joined up with him soon, hell would pop here in this mantrap of a station yard.

"Here!" Esmeralda tossed the reins of the horse she'd saddled for Longarm.

He caught them, unlatched the gate, and kicked it wide. Arlis was already mounted on a coyote dun. Esmeralda swung into the saddle of her rangy roan and squeezed the horse into a trot on out of the corral. Arlis followed, both women glancing toward the cabin as more rifles popped.

"Head east and keep your heads down," Longarm said, quickly closing and latching the gate. "I'll be along in a second. No matter what or who you see over there, keep riding!"

The station house's front door opened. Jackson stepped out with his rifle. He came to the edge of the porch and jerked a hand over his shoulder, narrowing one eye. "They're both pinned down. I think you're good for now!"

Longarm swung into the saddle of his buckskin, glanced at the butte pushing up northwest of the cabin. A man was scrambling down the side of the formation—a shadowy figure holding a rifle one-handed. He'd probably seen the girls gallop on out of the yard to the east. He was a good two hundred yards away—too far away for accurate shooting.

Longarm pointed the buckskin east and held the reins taut in his hands as he glanced at the stationmaster. "Thanks for the help, Jackson. You best get somewhere safe."

"I got a cellar dug for Injun attacks. They won't find me in there." He narrowed one eye. "I got a feelin' they'll be too hard after you to worry about me, though."

Longarm pinched his hat brim at the man and dug heels into the buckskin's flanks. The horse lurched forward, tearing off at a ground-eating run. In moments he was into the trees. The girls had slowed for him, regarding him anxiously, holding their prancing beasts taut-reined.

Longarm galloped past them. "Let's go!"

He passed the dead bounty hunters twisting lazily in the afternoon breeze, the dead men dappled by sunlight filtering through the cottonwood's crown. The buckskin leaped the creek with a great squawk of shifting leather and a loud rattle of bridle chains, and then Longarm put the horse up the cut between the buttes—the same cut the last man he'd killed had been heading for. He glanced back. Arlis was hard on his trail, leaning forward in her saddle. Esmeralda was about ten yards behind, rump pounding her saddle as she glanced warily over her shoulder.

From the direction of the station yard, rifles popped—several furious reports that ripped through the sunny afternoon quiet, the echoes vaulting off the surrounding buttes.

One slug puffed dust on the shoulder of the ridge to Esmeralda's right, blowing up rocks. The Mexican turned forward, flinching, and hunkered low as she ground her heels into her roan's flanks. The shot had to have been triggered by the man Longarm had seen from the yard, scrambling down the butte. He'd likely hightailed it upstream to try and cut off Longarm's and the girls' retreat.

Longarm crouched low and put the buckskin up the twisting cut between the buttes. To his right, a rattlesnake skittered down off the rock it had been sunning on and slithered into a long crack in the side of a gravelly incline, angrily flicking its rattle.

A quarter mile from the station house, the trail rose onto a flat-topped bench, then ribboned off over the bench toward a ragged-ridged jog of high, limestone bluffs that stretched from north to south across the horizon. Longarm turned the buckskin off the trail and slipped down from the saddle. As he dipped a hand into his saddlebags, the girls approached in a dusty swelter of blowing horses and clacking hooves.

"Keep going," he yelled, pulling a pair of army-issue field glasses from his saddlebag pouch. "I'll catch up to you."

"*Mierda!*" Esmeralda cursed as she batted her heels against her roan's ribs.

Arlis's horse curveted alongside the trail, as she turned her head toward Longarm. "What're you gonna do?"

"Take a gander at the station house." He waved her on. "Ride!"

When both girls had thudded on up the trail across the bench, Longarm strode quickly up a low hill of crumbling, striated limestone. He walked out onto a saucer-shaped ledge, on which a single dead cedar shrub drooped, and dropped to both knees. He removed the hide covers from the glasses and raised them to his face, adjusting the focus until the station house swam into view beyond the line of cottonwoods with their grisly cargo of dead bounty hunters.

Dust rose from the yard. Longarm adjusted the focus further, until several riders were clarified in the twin spheres of magnified vision. With a sickening feeling, he realized he'd been right the first time. Sager had been waiting for the imminent showing of the rest of his gang. Longarm and the girls hadn't taken leave of the place a moment too soon.

What about Jackson?

Longarm gritted his teeth and continued to adjust the focus. All he could bring into view was a mess of billowing yellow dust, prancing horses, and men in high-crowned hats and dusters milling around the yard. There were a good half dozen.

It looked like Sager was scouring the place for the stationmaster. If Jackson were well hidden, as he'd indicated he would be, the killers probably wouldn't waste much time looking for him. They had bigger fish to fry—namely, Longarm, Arlis Pine, and Esmeralda.

The thought had no sooner flicked across his mind than he heard a distant scream from the direction of the station house. He jerked the glasses with a start, disrupting his view of the yard. His pulse quickened as he readjusted the focus until he could see two men emerging from the cabin—one behind the other. The first man had long, gray hair. The man behind him raised his leg, and Jackson stumbled forward into the yard, falling against one of the killers' horses. He dropped to his knees, cottony hair blowing.

Longarm lowered the glasses, the rugged plains of his face hardening, his nostrils tightening. Jackson had been wrong about the safety of his hiding place. Sager had found him. Now they'd try to find out where Longarm was headed, and probably put a bullet through Jackson's brainpan.

Longarm's heart thudded heavily. The man had given him and the girls brief sanctuary. Longarm owed him. The girls could make it on their own if they kept riding.

As another scream tore across the buttes to mingle ominously among the sporadic buzzing of flies, Longarm ran back down the incline. He stopped near his horse, looking east. Both Arlis and Esmeralda had stopped their horses only twenty yards down the trail.

Rage burned like a wildfire through the lawman's veins. "I told you two . . ."

He let his voice trail off. Something was wrong. Esmeralda was hunkered nearly to her saddle horn on the other side of Arlis. Arlis turned toward him. Her face was shaded by her hat, but he could still see the look of anxiety there.

"Esmeralda took a bullet!"

Chapter 18

Longarm swung into the leather and galloped over to the other side of Esmeralda. The Mexican straightened, clutching her lower right side.

"*Mierda!*" she spat out furiously, scrunching her face with pain.

Longarm placed a hand on the back of her neck. "How bad?"

"It just clipped my side. I'll be all right."

Blood oozed between her fingers and dribbled down across her wide, brown belt. Longarm's pulse beat a war rhythm in his ears. He looked back toward the station house, which he couldn't see for the buttes bulging in front of him.

Inwardly, he cursed over and over. He couldn't ride off and leave the girls now. It was probably too late for Jackson, anyway. He'd best stick to the plan.

He looked at Esmeralda. "Can you ride?"

"*Sí, sí!*"

"You sure? I can pull you onto my horse."

She shook her dark head vehemently. "No. We couldn't make any time that way. I can ride." Her eyes flashed angry defiance. "So, let's ride, damnit!"

Longarm glanced at Arlis, then reined the buckskin around and put it into a gallop across the bench, heading toward the shaggy-crested hills in the far distance— maybe five, seven miles away. They were brown humps against the horizon, capped with pale chunks of limestone and tufts of green that were probably trees.

Longarm followed a meandering horse trail around the buttes and then out across a broad alkali flat peppered with cactus and a scattering of rocks. Not much grew out here, though there were a few mummified buffalo pies. Here and there a shallow, gravelly cut swerved toward him.

He glanced behind. Arlis was bringing up the rear in case Esmeralda couldn't make it. The Mexican was making a good fight of it, sitting almost straight in her saddle, chin dipped a little. Her pitted cheeks were taut with pain. Longarm wondered how many miles they could go before she toppled. He'd like to get at least as far as the first jog of low hills, maybe two miles away, before they stopped and tended her wound.

A rifle cracked. The report was almost inaudible. If it hadn't been for a momentary lull in the breeze, he likely wouldn't have heard it. It had come from behind. Longarm turned to peer that way now as the buckskin climbed through a crease between rocky knolls.

In the eastern distance, beyond the pale bluffs, charcoal smoke rose nearly straight up against the faultless blue sky. Longarm winced. Sager had set fire to the station house. The rifle report had likely been the end of Jackson. Again, Longarm cursed and ground his balled fist against his thigh.

He should have made the old man come along . . .

When they got into the first stretch of broken country that rose toward the limestone hills marking the breaks of Skull River, Longarm reined the buckskin to a halt and slipped out of his saddle. He ground-tied the reins and turned to where Esmeralda rode toward him, crouching lower now, chin dipped nearly to her chest. Her hat hung down her back by a horsehair thong, and her hair obscured her face.

He grabbed the roan's bit, stopping the beast, as the Mexican didn't seem able to pull back on the reins. Arlis rode up alongside her and stopped, leaning forward to look into Esmeralda's sweat-glistening face.

"Shit," muttered the Cross Fire girl. "She don't look good, Longarm."

The lawman reached up and eased Esmeralda out of her saddle. She fought him weakly. "What are you doing? I was going fine."

"Like hell. You were about to pass out."

Holding Esmeralda in his arms, Longarm kicked dirt up around a rock that stood tall as a chair, scaring off any snakes. Then he crouched and gentled the Mexican down to the ground, easing her back against the rock. She groaned when he probed the wound. It had more than just creased her side but appeared to have gone clean through, from back to front.

He grabbed her shirt in both his hands, ripped it open to halfway up her torso.

"*Cristo*!" she half-groaned, half-laughed. "I don't think we have time for this, lawman!"

Longarm stripped off his bandanna and stuffed it against the wound.

"Ah, shit—now you're trying to keel me? Make up your mind!"

"Hold that there. Press hard."

He took her own bandanna from around her neck and, leaning her forward, dabbed at the entrance wound. It wasn't bleeding as badly as the front exit wound.

He straightened and looked behind him. The smoke had grown thicker as it curled against the sky. Arlis had followed his gaze and looked back at him now, arching a brow. She knew what he was thinking. Having killed Jackson and set the way station ablaze, Sager was on his way.

Longarm helped Esmeralda to her feet. "You're gonna ride with me. I'll trail your horse."

"Ah, hell—I can ride . . ."

"Once we get into rougher country, we'll find a place to hole up and patch those wounds."

He picked her up in his arms and hefted her onto his saddle. Arlis held her steady with one hand, leaning out from her own horse, while Longarm grabbed the roan's reins and swung up behind the Mexican. He slid down over the cantle and sort of drew her across his lap.

"Ah," Esmeralda said through a lusty sigh, grinding her rump against his crotch. She leaned back and placed a hand on his unshaven cheek. "Nissss . . . lawman."

"Time an' a place for everything, senorita . . ."

He rammed his heels against the buckskin's ribs, and the horse lurched forward and up a knoll, heading into higher country in which a few patches of short grass soon appeared. They'd ridden about two miles from where Longarm and Esmeralda had started riding double when Arlis said, "Look!"

Longarm glanced behind. Chalky dust rose from a gray flat a mile away. Several small, brown blurs—Sager's men—were pulling the individual dust clouds along behind them. They were galloping hard, coming fast. Longarm counted seven.

He turned forward and whipped his rein ends against the buckskin's right wither, urging more speed. Up and over the low but ever-steepening hills they galloped. Soon they were climbing the abrupt slopes of the Skull Buttes, weaving around limestone outcroppings that ran at angles down from the sawtooth crests. Between the sheer escarpments that ran between twenty and fifty high were stunt cedars and scrub brush. Notch caves lined the bottoms of the outcroppings. Longarm, holding Esmeralda on his saddle before him, looked for a good place to hole up with the girls and patch her wounds.

A good place, too, from where he could see Sager's bunch as it approached. High, easily held ground was what he was looking for.

He found it near the crest of the long ridge—a cave with an oval opening. It was protected on two sides by spine-like ridges of pale rock streaked with granite and sandstone in which tiny fish and leaf fossils shone, as though they'd been chiseled there by the most delicate of ancient hands. Shrubs grew up along the bases of the formations. Longarm saw the cavern, then swerved the buckskin left, heading for it up the broad corridor of rock. Just beneath the opening, he sawed back on the buckskin's reins, swung down from the saddle, then let Esmeralda, who was now nearly unconscious, sag into his arms.

He turned to Arlis coming up behind him, her horse blowing and rolling its white-ringed eyes. Jerking his head toward some shrubs shaded by a ridge wall, he said, "Tie the horses in there. Loosen their saddle cinches and slip their bits, but leave 'em saddled."

Arlis looked weary and dusty—too tired to ask any questions. She half-fell from her saddle, letting her boots plop down in the dust, then grabbed the roan's and buckskin's reins and led them over to the shrubs sloping sharply down the side of the bluff, along the spine-like ridge of cracked and time-blasted rock.

Longarm strode up through a gravel slide beneath the cavern and climbed up around the lip of the opening before gaining the broad ledge in front of it. Pausing with Esmeralda hanging slack in his arms, he looked into the darkness, feeling the cool, dry caress of the air. Gradually, his eyes adjusted to the dimness, and he could see the pitted and fissured back wall. Swallows squeaked indignantly, looking out of their cone-shaped mud nests with their glinting gold eyes. They lifted a din at the unexpected intruder, and several flew out around him, a few propelling themselves at him like missiles, veering away at the last second.

Quickly, Longarm set Esmeralda down against the right wall of the cave. Her eyelids fluttered and her breasts rose and fell heavily. She'd lost the bandanna he'd given her to stem the blood loss, and the blood had dribbled thickly down over her belt and onto her upper right thigh.

He called for Arlis to bring his saddlebags and rifle, and when the girl brought the gear, he quickly went to work hauling out gauze bandages and a bottle of whiskey. He also laid out a clean linen cloth, then looked at Arlis, who'd dropped to one knee beside Esmeralda, smoothing the Mexican's sweat-soaked hair back from her forehead.

"You ever cleaned a wound before?"

Arlis nodded.

"Clean both her entrance and exit wounds out good with whiskey then wrap 'em with gauze. I'm gonna go down and meet our friends trailin' us."

"You're gonna need help."

Longarm looked into Arlis's sharp, hazel eyes. "You stay here with Esmeralda. No matter what."

Softly, she said, "What if you don't come back?"

Longarm doffed his hat and ran a hand through his hair. Putting his hat back on his head, he drew a deep breath. "You have your rifles. Take out as many of 'em as you can. Then . . ."

He tucked his bottom lip under the top one and gave her a pointed, meaningful look.

Arlis understood. She nodded. "Be careful. When you kill Sager, tell him it's for Alvin and Arlis Pine from the Cross Fire Ranch out of Lightning Flat, Wyoming." She narrowed her eyes. "Make him die hard, Longarm."

The lawman smiled, pressed his thumb against the girl's dimpled chin, then rose and left the cave.

Chapter 19

Longarm booted the buckskin down the side of the mountain. He reined up about halfway down, in a little depression behind a wagon-sized boulder that had a gaping, crooked crack in it. From the crack, a cedar grew, offering shade and cover.

The lawman swung down from his saddle and dropped the buckskin's reins. He slid his rifle from its scabbard and, running his hand up and down the smooth walnut forestock, climbed the knoll and hunkered down behind the boulder from which the cedar grew. A blackbird lighted from a branch of the gnarled tree and winged off, squawking. Longarm gritted his teeth at the bird's noise—the damn thing might give him away—then doffed his hat as he stretched a look over the top of the boulder.

Six riders loped toward him across the dun flat mottled with greasewood and cactus. Alkali dust rose to waver above them like a thin, brown curtain against the brassy sky. Gunmetal and brass cartridges winked in the sunlight. Longarm's pulse quickened, and he hunkered lower, keeping his eyes just above the edge of the boulder, as he slowly racked a fresh shell into his Winchester's breech.

"Come on, Sager." Longarm hardened his eyes, remembering the rifle report he'd heard from the direction of the Skull Butte way station and the smoke he'd seen rise. "Come on and meet your maker, you sonofabitch."

It had been a long trail. The big lawman was nearly at the end of it. And he'd rarely run down an outlaw more deserving to die than Del Sager. The number of men the man had killed was too great to count. But Alvin Pine and the stationmaster, Jackson, would be his last.

Longarm's eyes fairly blazed above the sun-bleached boulder, beneath an arm of the cedar, as he watched the six horses gallop toward him, heads bobbing, dust rising, the thuds of their pounding hooves gradually growing louder. They were within a hundred and fifty yards and closing. Between them and Longarm lay a rocky hill a little beneath his elevation. When they'd crested that hill and started down, heading toward him, they'd be well within range.

That's when he'd cut down on them.

No warning shots or pleas for the bastards to throw their weapons down. None of that bullshit. Even if Longarm hadn't had the girls to worry about, one of them wounded, he wouldn't have given Sager's men that much of a chance. That would be a foolish, tinhorn move— one lawman against six of the gnarliest killers he'd ever stood against. No one would expect it from him, either. Certainly not Billy Vail, who'd been out here when things were even wilder, if that were possible, and knew by how thin a thread a lawman's life always hung.

You weighed the odds and placed the safest bet possible.

Now he caressed the hammer of his cocked rifle with his right thumb, feeling the electricity of expectation trill through his nerves. The riders disappeared on the other side of the hill, but he could see their dust continue to rise as they climbed it, continuing on toward Longarm at a horse-killing pace.

Longarm shifted around behind the rock, shoving his left shoulder up hard against it, making himself more comfortable. He ground his heels into the loose sand and gravel at the boulder's base, felt the coolness of the rock through his clothes. It was a good feeling. It seemed to buoy his spirits a bit, give him confidence.

Sager's trail was ending here. He wouldn't get him, Longarm, and he wouldn't get the girls.

One rider appeared at the crest of the opposite hill. Then another and another, and as the hooves of their horses thudded loudly, shoes clacking off rocks and spewing gravel, all six plunged down the hill toward Longarm, the horses' shoulders lunging forward over their grinding hooves.

Longarm stood. Sager was on the far right. He'd take the others first—one at a time, like shooting bottles and airtight tins off fence posts.

Narrowing his right eye, causing deep, red lines to spoke out from its leathery corner, the lawman took up the slack in his trigger finger.

Boom!

The rider on the far left jerked suddenly as though he'd been stung by a bee, but his horse kept on galloping down the slope. Longarm ejected the smoking cartridge casing from the rifle, heard it clatter onto the gravel behind him, then rammed a fresh one into the breech. The second rider in line had just started to saw back on his horse's reins when Longarm's rifle thundered again. The first man had just tumbled out of his saddle as the second man sagged back against his galloping horse's rump, throwing his arms straight up above his head and flopping there as though his bones had turned to jelly. His head and shoulders slid down off his horse's right hip but held there, as both his boots were caught in the stirrups and his body had nowhere to go.

His horse, feeling the odd shifting of its rider's weight as well as smelling his blood, acquired a hitch in its gallop and loosed a shrill whinny.

Boom!

The third rider was holding his reins in one hand. He'd just gotten his own rifle yanked from its scabbard and was raising the piece one-handed, when Longarm's round hammered dust from his left shoulder.

The man jerked sideways and dropped his rifle as he slapped his right hand to the wound. A half second later, his horse plunged forward on its knees and rolled. The horse and rider disappeared in a small dust storm through which Longarm glimpsed flailing hooves and a flying hat before, grinding his teeth, he seated a fresh round and swung his attention to the fourth man.

He and the fifth man and Del Sager—distinguishable by his long black beard, black hat, and gray duster—were all angling their horses toward Longarm's right as they reached the bottom of the hill. Sager was cocking his Winchester one-handed and shouting. The man next in Longarm's killing line was staring toward Longarm and also shouting as he took his reins in his teeth. He took quick aim from his mount's jostling back and fired, the slug kicking up rocks and gravel near the base of Longarm's covering boulder.

"Longarm!" The girl's shout came from behind him.

Levering a fresh round, Longarm swung around to see Arlis standing high on a limestone ridge behind and above him about fifty yards. She swung an arm out, waving her pistol in the air. As she started running down the pinnacle, Longarm stood and shouted furiously, "Get back to the cave—goddamnit, girl!"

A rifle thundered behind him, from the direction of Sager's riders, and a ricochet screamed off the top of the boulder to snap a slender branch from the cedar. Longarm crouched but kept his head up far enough to peer over the boulder. A man with a long, red beard and an old, torn Confederate campaign hat was storming up Longarm's knoll, flapping his arms like wings. His yellow eyes were bright with killing fury, and he aimed a carbine in one hand, a long-barreled Colt in the other.

Longarm ducked as both the rifle and the Colt exploded.

The slugs screeched over the top of Longarm's head, one clipping an edge of the boulder and peppering his cheek and jaw with stone slivers. The horse's hammering hooves hammered louder. Longarm jerked his head and rifle up and pulled the trigger.

Boom!

The horse whinnied shrilly as it veered sharply to

Longarm's right. For an instant, the rider sat with his
back straight, dropping his weapons down both sides of
the horse and reaching for the blood-jetting hole in his
throat. He grimaced, showing teeth so yellow that they
were almost brown inside the grimy red beard. Before
he could grab his throat, the horse's sudden swerve threw
the rider down the animal's left stirrup fender.

The horse continued to swing wide of Longarm.

As it did, it sprayed rocks and gravel against the base
of the boulder. It also swung its rider, whose right boot
had gotten hung up in its stirrup, against the side of the
boulder, the man's head connecting with a dull, wet, crack-
ing sound. The air exploded from the man's lungs as the
horse galloped westward along the shoulder of the slope,
dragging the flopping, bloody, dead rider along behind it.

Longarm scowled as he racked another round. He
looked for Sager, but there were only dead men out here,
the only movements the riderless horses galloping cra-
zily this way and that as they fled the smell of powder
smoke and bloody death.

Longarm glanced behind him. Arlis was gone.

Thumbing fresh cartridges into his Winchester, he ran
down the knoll to his horse that stood wide-eyed, its tail
arched at the recent cacophony. Grabbing the reins, he
shoved the rifle into its scabbard. Somewhere behind
him, on the other side of a limestone ridge, hooves thudded. There was the pop of a small-caliber pistol. A girl
screamed.

Gooseflesh rose down Longarm's sweaty back. He
swung up into the saddle and rammed heels against the
horse's flanks, lurching up the opposite slope and around
the base of the ridge on which he'd last seen Arlis. He

topped the ridge, the horse blowing, and caught a glimpse of a black-hatted man a half-second before smoke puffed around the figure.

The pistol's pop reached Longarm's ears at the same time the buckskin screamed and convulsed. Arlis screamed again. As the horse twisted, its legs giving, Longarm saw Del Sager holding Arlis on a low, rocky ridge about fifty yards up the next incline. He had one arm around the girl's neck, pulling her taut against him. His hat was gone. In Sager's other hand he held a black-barreled revolver.

He pulled the girl back down over the ridge as the buckskin collapsed, and Longarm kicked free of the stirrups as he threw himself to the left and went rolling down the side of the ridge away from Sager and Arlis.

"Fuck!" he grated out, digging his heels and elbows into the knoll to stop his fall.

He climbed to his feet and scrambled back up the hill. On the opposite ridge, Sager and Arlis were gone. Longarm grabbed his Winchester from the saddle boot, yanking it out from under the dead horse. Sager's bullet had drilled the poor beasts's skull.

The lawman wiped the dust and sand from the receiver. He looked around, but all he could see of Sager was dust rising from behind the opposite ridge. The killer was riding up the hill toward the cave, but the limestone outcrops blocked him from Longarm's view. He was going to use Arlis and Esmeralda as bait to draw Longarm in, the same way Longarm had used Little Louis to lure Sager.

Longarm looked around for a horse, but the horses of Sager's bunch had all run off, only dust sifting behind them. Anxiety a dead weight in his belly, Longarm jogged up the opposite ridge, curving around the shoulder and into the ravine on the other side. He saw where Sager's horse had torn chunks out of the wiry brown grass and thin soil. He was riding double with Arlis, following Longarm's and the girls' own recent trail, heading for that damn cave where he'd find Esmeralda.

Raking air in and out of his tired lungs, Longarm jogged up the hill between the towering ridges of limestone. The sun hammered him, reflecting off the pale rocks. Flies buzzed in the tall grass and shrubs along the bases of the ridges. Otherwise, the silence was like that just before a powderkeg erupts.

He almost wished he'd hear something, anything, from the direction of the cave. By now, Sager had likely made it there with Arlis and was doing God knew what to both girls.

Suddenly, he did hear something. A girl shouting in Spanish.

Esmeralda!

His lungs aching as though they'd both been speared, Longarm rounded a bend in the corridor he'd been following.

And saw the cave.

He blinked once, twice, three times. Esmeralda sat on the ledge before the cave, dangling her legs over the side. Below the ledge and under a tall cottonwood that grew up from the base of the ridge on Longarm's right, a horse sat. A rider sat the horse. A rope dangled from a low branch just above the rider's head. The rope was wrapped around the rider's neck.

Another figure, blurry from Longarm's distance, stood near the horse's right hip. Sager had his hands on his hips as he stared down the steep, gravelly slope toward Longarm.

Waiting for Longarm to join the hanging party.

As though he'd been punched in the belly, Longarm's breath gushed out of his lungs. Sager was going to hang Arlis!

"Sager, goddamn you!"

Longarm ran a few more yards, then stopped suddenly. He stared up the slope. Esmeralda was shouting encouragement in Spanish, pumping one fist in the air while holding her wounded side with her other hand. Longarm looked at Sager standing beside the horse. Only it wasn't Sager. He'd thought it was Sager because of the light and the angle and because the figure wasn't wearing a hat.

But Arlis was standing beside the horse, her hands on her hips. Her pistol poked up from behind her belt, the barrel jammed into her pants over her belly.

Sager sat his horse, the noose around his neck. His shoulders slumped forward, as though he'd been injured. Had Arlis managed to shoot him, get the upper hand?

As the confusion lifted like fog from Longarm's brain, his heart lightened, though his lungs continued aching as he climbed the slope. He stopped about twenty yards downhill from Arlis, who stared at him hard, lips pursed. Esmeralda had stopped yelling and now looked down the incline at Longarm. She was smiling.

"Longarm!" Sager spat, voice tense, his eyes darting down as if to consider the rope knotted around his neck. "Don't let her do this! Don't let this little bitch do this to me!"

Arlis kept her eyes on Longarm. Quietly, she said,

"What do you say we give this bastard his just desserts?"

Longarm slid his gaze from Arlis to Esmeralda. The Mexican's eyes were wide though their corners were spoked with pain.

"Longarm!" Sager shouted. "This ain't right! This here's vigilante justice. Don't let these little bitches do this to me!"

Longarm drew a deep breath and lowered his rifle, letting the barrel hang toward the ground. To Arlis he said, "What're you askin' me for? I'm still down there, headin' this way. Doubt I'll make it in time to ever find out what the hell happened up here."

He stretched his longhorn mustache in a devilish half smile.

Arlis returned it.

Del Sager's dark eyes blazed. "*Longarm!*"

Arlis slid her pistol from her pants, cocked the hammer back.

"Longarm!" Sager cried, his voice echoing around the ridges.

Arlis raised the gun above her shoulder.

"Longarm, damn y—"

Bam!

The horse ran out from under the tree, racing past Longarm in a curtain of rising dust.

Del Sager's neck snapped like a dry twig.

Esmeralda clapped.

Arlis sat down heavily and looked up at the twisting, dying man in unabashed delight. "That's for my pa, Alvin Pine, you son of a bitch!"

Longarm shouldered his rifle and climbed the slope.

Arlis was sobbing. Esmeralda said nothing, her expression suddenly somber. While Sager twitched in the air, barely alive and dying fast, the lawman sat down beside Arlis and wrapped the crying girl in his arms.

Watch for

LONGARM AND THE COLD CASE

the 392nd novel in the exciting LONGARM
series from Jove

Coming in July!

GIANT-SIZED ADVENTURE FROM AVENGING ANGEL LONGARM.

BY TABOR EVANS

penguin.com/actionwesterns

M456AS0510

DON'T MISS A YEAR OF

Slocum Giant
by
Jake Logan

penguin.com/actionwesterns

M457AS0510

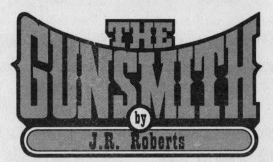